THE HOUSE ON SUNRISE LAGOON

BOOK THREE

Halfway to Harbor

THE HOUSE ON SUNRISE LAGOON

BOOK THREE

Halfway to Harbor

NICOLE MELLEBY

ALGONQUIN YOUNG READERS   2024

Published by
Algonquin Young Readers
an imprint of Workman Publishing Co., Inc.,
a subsidiary of Hachette Book Group, Inc.
1290 Avenue of the Americas
New York, New York 10104

Printed in the United States of America. Design by Neil Swaab.

The publisher is not responsible for websites (or their content)
that are not owned by the publisher.

LIBRARY OF CONGRESS CATALOGING-IN-PUBLICATION DATA

[TK]

ISBN 978-1-64375-312-6 (hardcover)
ISBN 978-1-5235-2724-3 (paperback)

10 9 8 7 6 5 4 3 2 1
First Edition

DEDICATION TO COME

THE HOUSE ON SUNRISE LAGOON

BOOK THREE

Halfway to Harbor

THE THIRD RULE OF BOATING:
KNOW WHEN TO GET OUT OF THE WAY.

Her dad was there, too. Not with the rest of her family—he stood alone on the side of the court by the edge of the bleachers. He didn't cheer loudly. He didn't really cheer at all. He stood there, and occasionally called out things like, "Plant your feet!" and "Nice follow through!" and all the other things he'd taught her about how to play basketball in the first place.

But even though he wasn't loud like the rest of her family, that didn't mean she liked having him there. She didn't. It was distracting to see him standing to one the side while her moms and siblings sat on the opposite side. She sometimes wondered if it was also weird for him, or weird for Mom, or weird for Mama. Maybe it was weird for her siblings to know Harbor had a dad who wasn't *their* dad, who was at the game watching her play, too.

"Harbor, pay attention!" That was her dad, and Harbor did snap to attention, but not before noticing Mom had turned her head to glance over at her dad.

Someone passed Harbor the ball, and she planted her giant feet and reached up to take the shot. The girl who tried to block Harbor was much smaller than she was and smacked Harbor on the arm instead of hitting the basketball. The referee blew his whistle again, but this time it was good news. This time it was Harbor who would get to take the foul shots.

The gymnasium hushed as Harbor lined up her foul shot, and she relished in it. She closed her eyes and listened to the silence—a rare moment of quiet.

But then Cordelia yelled, "Go, Harbor!"

And Mom said, "Go, Harbor!" too.

And her dad said, "Don't forget to follow through."

And Mama said, "You've got this!"

And Harbor wondered what it would be like to have a family that wasn't so complicated or distracting.

Harbor missed both her foul shots. Luckily, her team still won. Even luckier, her coach didn't reprimand her for missing those foul shots and focused instead on all the good things Harbor had done.

Their coach dismissed them, and Harbor gathered her gym bag and water bottle. Since wrangling the Ali-O'Connor family was an ordeal, Harbor wasn't surprised her dad was the first one to meet her. "Good game, kid," he said.

"Thanks, Dad."

"We'll practice those foul shots next time you come over. You just gotta get used to your extra height," he said, putting a hand on the top of her head to emphasize all her brand-new inches. He gave her a wink, and she smiled.

People always said Harbor looked like her mom. It was true. They both were blond and they both were tall, though Harbor was now taller. But when Harbor stood next to her dad, she looked the most like him, too. They had the same nose and the same eyes. Sometimes Harbor wondered what other people would see if the three of them were still a family unit and stood together more often. Maybe they'd say she looked like *both* of them.

It didn't matter, though, because they—her mom, her dad, and Harbor—rarely stood together.

Especially since Harbor was usually surrounded by her siblings, none of whom looked like her, most of whom didn't even look like one another, anyway, besides the twins of course. The Ali-O'Connor family was a hodgepodge of different genes— Harbor was Mom's biological daughter; the twins were Mama's and a donor. Sam and Marina were both adopted.

Realizing they were taking longer than normal, Harbor looked around. "Do you know where Mom went?"

"I think they all ran to the bathroom. Hey," her dad said, turning around to poke the shoulder of a woman who was chatting with one of Harbor's teammates and her parents. "I want you to meet someone. Dawn, I want you to meet Harbor."

Dawn was a tall—the kind of tall that made Harbor feel small—Black woman with big dark eyes and an even bigger smile. "Ah, here's your girl. You played quite a game, Harbor."

"Thanks," Harbor squeaked out, not really in the mood for small talk—especially if this woman turned out to be her dad's new girlfriend. He didn't often date, but when he did, Harbor never really knew how to act around the women he dated.

"Really," Dawn said. "You're exceptionally talented." She turned to Harbor's dad and placed a hand on his shoulder. Harbor tried not to make a face. "I have to get going, but it was really great getting to see you. I'll be in touch, okay?"

"Sounds good. See you later, Dawn."

"Bye," she said. "And bye, Harbor! Hope to see you real soon."

Harbor wasn't sure what to make of that.

She didn't have time to dwell on it, though, because no sooner was Dawn walking away than two little arms were wrapping themselves around her waist, Cordelia's body slamming into Harbor's back in a bear hug. "Harbor! You played so good! Did you hear me cheering for you? My throat hurts now!"

"Yeah, I bet," Harbor mumbled.

Lir joined in on the bear hug from the front, making Harbor the middle of a twin-sandwich. "Did you hear us?"

Harbor looked up as the rest of her family, plus Boom, made their way over. She glared at Mama as she said, "Yep. I heard you loud and clear."

Mama laughed. "Will you believe me if I told you I *did* tell them to take it down a notch or two?"

"I wouldn't believe you, and I was there when you told us," Marina chimed in.

"I totally get why you like that intense-looking WNBA player on the poster in your room," Boom said. "Your face gets all scary and intense just like hers!"

"Thanks, I think."

"Oh, it's definitely a compliment," Boom clarified. She held up her phone. "I got all your baskets on camera. Even the ones you missed."

Boom, annoyingly, always got *everything* on camera.

"Let me through so I can see my little fish," Mom said, squeezing her way around everyone else. She wrapped her arms around Harbor. Harbor was a little taller than Mom these days, and when Mom rested her head against Harbor's, Harbor liked having that extra height. It felt really nice.

"Our kid isn't really a little fish anymore," Harbor's dad said.

Harbor had almost forgotten he was still there.

Mom pulled back to look at him. "She'll be my little fish no matter how big she gets."

"Can we go home now? Everyone else left already," Harbor said. The gym was basically empty, but her entire family made it still feel plenty crowded. Plenty loud, too.

"Yeah, come on," Mom said. "Let's get out of here, I'm starving."

"Mama said we could get pizza!" Cordelia said.

"You're welcome to join us at the house for dinner if you'd like, Doug." It was Mama who invited Harbor's dad along. She was always the one to be the most cordial. Whenever Mom and Harbor's dad fought, it was Mama who tried to play peacekeeper.

Mom didn't look thrilled as she said, "Yeah, sure, come have pizza with us."

"Do you like pineapple on your pizza, Doug?" Lir asked. "We've never had pineapple on our pizza, but we really want to try it."

"Our friend Pork says it's really good," Cordelia added. "It also has ham on it, that's what Pork says."

"Pork is a person?" Harbor's dad asked. "But the ham, that's on the pizza?"

"Yes, correct," Cordelia confirmed.

"I've never had pineapple on my pizza," Harbor's dad said. "And, unfortunately, I won't be able to try it with you tonight. I should get home."

"You sure?" Mom said. "We're getting regular pizza, regardless of what the twins think."

"Hey!"

"What about pepperoni? Mama, you said we could get pepperoni," Marina said.

Harbor's head was starting to spin a bit. The gym really *was* empty now except for her family and the janitors. "We should go," Harbor said.

"Come here, kid." Harbor's dad pulled her in for a hug. "We'll practice together next time you come over, okay? You did great tonight." He gestured in Mom's direction, getting her attention. "Hey, I'll call you later, okay? I need to talk to you about something."

"Yeah, okay," Mom said.

Harbor was about to ask him what he needed to talk to Mom about, but before she could, he was pulling her in for another half-hug. "Okay, great, see you later, Harbor!" he said, walking away.

"All right, for real, we need to get going so they can lock up this gym," Mama said, ushering the rest of the family toward the exit.

Harbor's dad went one way, and the rest of the Ali-O'Connors went the other.

CHAPTER TWO

They did not get the pineapple pizza. Mama knew better. The twins liked their pizza plain—always just plain—and she didn't want to buy a pie no one would eat. Mom, Marina, and Sam chose pepperoni. Mama always ate whatever was left. Harbor, whose they were supposed to be celebrating, wasn't even consulted in the pizza-topping discussion.

"Can I have a fork and knife please?" Lir asked.

"For your pizza?" Mom looked as though Lir had sprouted an extra head.

"Yes. I don't like the pizza grease on my fingers."

"Only if you're careful with the knife. Go sit down, I'll bring it to you," Mama said. "Boom, plain or pepperoni?"

"Pepperoni, please!"

Boom was staying over for dinner because Boom was always over for dinner these days. Harbor thought they had enough

Ali-O'Connors without Marina inviting her best friend to practically be part of the family, but no one asked for her opinion. The only good thing about Boom staying for dinner was that it meant they got an entire extra pie. Which meant there would be extra slices.

Good Boy, the Ali-O'Connors' giant Great Dane, whined at the counter where Mama placed the pizza boxes. He was tall enough to rest his head on the counter and stare longingly at the food.

"Can I have one of each?" Sam asked.

"I remember when most of you kids would have two bites of a slice and Mama or I would have to finish the rest of it. The bigger you kids get, the more food you eat," Mom said.

"That's usually how growing works, yes," Mama said.

"Our poor bank account."

Cordelia, who couldn't do anything without making a mess, was pulling the cheese off her pizza in big clumps. One of those clumps hit the floor with a *splat*, and Good Boy nearly tripped over his own big feet to get to it before anyone could clean it up.

Harbor, who never thought she'd be able to relate to their giant slobbery dog, could absolutely relate to his giant, uncoordinated feet.

Sam was heading to her seat with both slices of her pizza when she glanced out the back window, ducking a little for a better view. "Sonny's outside. Can I ask if he wants some pizza?"

Harbor snapped her head to look out the window, too. "I'll do it," she said. Sam had hung out with Sonny while Harbor was at basketball practice the other day. Harbor felt a little weird about that.

She hadn't seen Sonny yet this summer since he'd started his break with a week-long baseball camp. And when he'd finally arrived, Harbor had been playing basketball. They hadn't crossed paths yet, which was weird for them. Even though Sonny and his two brothers only came to Sunrise Lagoon to stay with their grandparents for the summers, he and Harbor had been best friends for as long as she could remember.

She hadn't seen Sonny since Labor Day weekend last year.

"You should go wash up," Mom said, then added playfully, "You're a little rank."

"I'll wash up after dinner. I'm gonna go invite Sonny," Harbor said, and didn't wait for Mom to say if it was okay or not. She went out the back door and onto their deck. Harbor loved where the Ali-O'Connors lived, on Sunrise Lagoon—especially in the summer. Instead of a backyard, they had a deck that led to a dock, which looked out on the water. A lagoon separated Sonny's grandparents' house from Harbor's, and they had spent many summers swimming and kayaking and crabbing in that lagoon together.

She wasn't allowed to run on the back deck—Mom had a lot of rules about living on the water—so she walked only as fast as she thought her mom would allow. She stood in between her mom's boats that were tied up on the dock so that she could see Sonny. He was hosing down the Badgers' kayaks.

"Hey."

Sonny looked up. When he saw Harbor standing there, he turned his hose off. "Oh. Hey."

It was always a little weird when they first saw each other after an entire school year. They spent almost every day together in the summers but missed birthdays and holidays and growth spurts the rest of the year.

"Hi," Harbor said again.

"How was your game?" Sonny asked.

"We won," Harbor said.

"Oh cool."

"Yeah."

"I guess you grew a lot?" Sonny said. "I mean! It looks like you grew a lot?"

Even from her view here, he didn't seem to have grown at all. She was probably a lot taller than Sonny now.

"Do you want to come over for pizza?"

Sonny shook his head. "I already ate? Sorry."

"It's okay."

"Maybe next time?"

"Yeah, okay." Harbor didn't know what else to say. The sun was starting to set. It felt nice outside with the breeze. Harbor remembered how excited she was last year when the Badger brothers had arrived for the summer. She had immediately jumped in the lagoon to swim across and greet them. "You're washing the kayaks?"

"They've been in the shed since last year. They were so gross."

"Maybe we can use them tomorrow? If you want?"

Sonny shrugged. "Yeah, okay."

"Okay."

Harbor knew she should turn around and go inside for dinner. She needed to eat, and she still needed to shower. Still, she found herself lingering on the dock, watching as Sonny started up his hose again. None of this felt like it was supposed to. "I'll see you tomorrow then?" Harbor shouted.

Sonny turned off the hose again. "What?"

"I'll see you tomorrow? We can kayak?" Harbor asked.

"Oh. Yeah. Okay," Sonny said. "Sounds good."

Sonny started the hose again. Harbor went back inside.

CHAPTER THREE

Boom was sleeping over. Harbor had come back to her room after showering to find a sleeping bag on her bedroom floor. The bedroom was crowded enough already, since she shared it with both Marina and Sam.

"Can't you sleep in the living room or something?" Harbor scowled at Marina.

"I don't like sleeping anywhere except for here, in my bed, with my sound machine, and everything I am used to," Marina said.

Harbor's middle sister was anxious about a lot of things. Her moms said to give Marina a little patience, that she couldn't control all the things that worried her or stressed her out. Still, sometimes it bugged the heck out of Harbor anyway.

"I need my own room," Harbor mumbled, and not for the first time.

"I have my own room," Boom said from her usual spot on the bedroom floor. "And it's actually pretty lonely. There's no one to talk to there!"

"You're supposed to sleep in a bedroom, not talk."

"That's mighty boring, Harbor."

"Not everything needs to be one of your movies, Boom," Harbor fired back.

"Hey, be nice in here," Mama said as she entered the bedroom. She had an extra pillow in her hands that she handed over to Boom.

"We barely fit in this bedroom as is," Harbor said. "Boom has her own house and her own family."

"Boom is an honorary Ali-O'Connor," Marina said.

"We have enough Ali-O'Connors!"

Mama wrapped an arm around Harbor's shoulders. "Hey, come on. It's just tonight. Do you want to sleep somewhere else tonight instead? I can set you up by yourself in the living room? Or you can sleep with Mom and me?"

"Mom snores," Harbor said.

"I do not!" Mom said from somewhere out in the hallway.

"Yes you do!" Sam and Marina shouted from their beds while the twins both shouted the same thing from their room across the hall.

"We have no room in this house!" Harbor said. "You can't even have a conversation without someone overhearing it!"

"Hey, Harbor?" Mom poked her head in the bedroom. "Why don't you come into our room for a bit. Let your sisters and Boom settle in. We need to chat about something anyway."

Harbor groaned but let Mama lead her across the hall. Harbor loved their home—she loved living on the water, she loved the bird sanctuary across the way with all the ospreys and blue herons and egrets, and she loved Mom's three boats tied up to the dock in the lagoon out back. But their house, which only had three bedrooms and one bathroom, was too small for two moms, one giant dog, five kids, and, occasionally, their friends. Especially now that Harbor was older and taller. The house felt like it was shrinking.

Good Boy was on his dog bed on the floor of her moms' room. When he saw Harbor, he tried to roll over so she could pet his belly, but he misjudged just how close he was to the wall and his legs smacked against it with a thud. Harbor sat on the floor and Good Boy rolled over again, laid his head in her lap, and immediately started drooling as she rubbed his ears.

"Good Boy is too big for this house, too," Harbor said.

Mom sat on the edge of the bed, and Mama sat on the other side, spreading lotion on her legs and knees, her usual bedtime routine. "We can't really do anything about the size of the house right now, Harbor," Mom said. "Cut Marina and Boom some slack."

"It's my bedroom, too, and Boom is *always* in it."

"We'll try and limit their sleepovers each week," Mama said. "Okay?"

Harbor sighed. "Yeah. Fine."

"We actually wanted to talk to you about something else," Mom said. "Your dad called a little bit ago. He said he introduced you to his friend Dawn?"

Great. They were going to sit her down and tell her that her dad had a girlfriend. Harbor didn't really want to have this conversation. "Yeah. We talked for, like, two seconds."

"Did he tell you she's a basketball coach?"

"Um. No?"

"Well, she is. She coaches for an elite summer league, up by where your dad lives," Mom said.

"Oh." Harbor was a little confused. "She watched me play?"

Mom nodded. "She did."

"She thought you were excellent," Mama added.

"I missed my free throws."

"You still had a great game," Mama said.

Harbor shrugged. Mama wasn't really a basketball expert. Harbor could run back and forth and not score a single basket, and Mama would tell her she did wonderfully. "So . . . what did you and Dad talk about then?"

"Coach Dawn wants you to play for her this summer," Mom said. "Her summer team is a level up from where you're playing now, and if you want to keep improving, or if you want to play after high school—"

"Which you don't have to commit to now," Mama interrupted.

"Right, which you don't need to commit to now, but if you wanted to, this team could help you start to focus on that."

Harbor was so excited she hadn't realized she'd stopped petting Good Boy until he started to whine. "Wait, really? I want to! I mean, I really want to keep playing. I want to get better, and move up, and keep playing. Can I? Can I play on this team?"

Her moms exchanged glances.

"If it's what you really want," Mom said.

"It is! It definitely is."

"There's just one thing," Mom said. She started toying with the strings on her pajama pants, which was a telltale sign that she was nervous about something. Which made Harbor a little nervous, too.

"What?" she asked.

"It'd just be on the weekends. Long practice days, and the games in the evenings."

"That's fine!" Harbor said. It would give her all week to enjoy the summer on the lagoon, and hang with Sonny, without having to miss too much. "That's perfect!"

Mom stopped playing with her pajama strings. "You'd have to spend those weekends at your dad's."

Oh. "Every weekend?" Harbor asked. "All weekend?"

"It'd be too much for us to drive you back and forth. And your dad lives five minutes from the courts you'd be playing on," Mama said. "So one of us would take you over on Friday night and pick you up either Sunday night or Monday morning—we still need to work the details out a bit."

"Oh," Harbor said.

Harbor usually spent two weekends a month at her dad's house. Mostly. Sometimes they skipped a weekend or two if she had basketball or he had something to do or she had summer plans or birthday parties or whatever else. Their visits were more consistent when she was little, but they hadn't been consistent in a long time. And she'd never spent every single weekend with him.

"Mama!" Marina called from across the hall. "Can Boom and I borrow your laptop to watch a movie before bed!"

Immediately after, Cordelia and Lir poked their head into their moms' bedroom. "Can one of you come read with us before bed?" Lir asked.

And then Sam poked her head up behind them. With their bodies hidden behind the doorway, they looked like three floating heads stacked up on top of one another, with Sam on top. "Can I have another blanket? Marina put the fan on high and it's a little too chilly."

Then Good Boy suddenly got up, nudging Harbor a little to the side, and ran over to jump on and lick the twins. Her moms were already climbing out of bed. "I'll come read to you both in a minute," Mama was saying as Mom told Sam, "I'll grab a blanket for you and the laptop for your sister."

Harbor stayed on the floor of her moms' room and thought, *At least at my dad's house I have my own room.*

She could play basketball and have her own room *every single weekend.*

CHAPTER FOUR

Harbor wasn't a morning person. She liked to sleep, and she especially liked to sleep lately. It seemed like her body used all its energy to grow and she needed to make up for that by sleeping extra. Usually her family let her sleep. Mostly because she was pretty grumpy when she didn't.

Sometimes, though, she wished she *was* a morning person. This morning, with Boom breathing really loudly in her sleep, Sam tossing and turning and making her blankets rustle every five seconds, and Marina's sound machine loudly buzzing away, Harbor was awake before everyone. And, yes, she was grumpy, but she climbed out of bed anyway.

Good Boy didn't immediately run to greet her as she left her bedroom, which meant that at least one of her moms must already be awake and walking him. In the kitchen, the coffee pot was half full. Harbor looked around and spotted Mom on the back deck sitting in one of the Adirondack chairs, sipping her coffee. Harbor, still in her pajamas, went outside.

Mom was also still in her pajamas. "Wow. You're up early."

"Couldn't sleep," Harbor said. "Too much noise, too many—"

"People? Yeah, I know, Harbor. I hear you," Mom said. She quietly added, "I'm doing my best here."

It made Harbor feel a little guilty. Just last summer Mom had given up her boat repair business to work instead for Koch's Marina so she could have a steadier, better paycheck.

There was a second mug of coffee sitting on the table. "Where's Mama?" Harbor asked.

"Walking Good Boy," Mom said. "Hey, I was thinking about going fishing this afternoon. Do you want to come? Me, you, and Sam like usual?"

Last summer, Harbor would have jumped at the chance. "Nah. I'm going to see if Sonny wants to hang later."

"You sure?" Mom asked. "You could invite Sonny, if you wanted?"

"It's okay. I'm sure."

Mom kept her eyes on Harbor for a moment, for long enough that Harbor was about to tell her to knock it off. Her cheeks felt warm. The sun was already strong enough, though, so it could have just been the summer heat.

"Come sit with me," Mom said, patting what was certainly supposed to be Mama's chair.

Harbor came around to sit anyway. She'd get up whenever Mama got there.

"You know, I remember the first time I took you on a boat," Mom suddenly said. "You were just a baby. This little wrinkly thing. Any time the water spritzed your face, you'd wave your little arms around, all angry. Like you were picking a fight with the sea. Your grandpa, I'm not sure if you remember him, he was driving the boat. And your dad was there, too. The life vest looked so big on you. You were so small then."

"I'm not so small anymore," Harbor said.

Mom kept looking at her. "No. I guess you're not."

"Did we do that a lot?" Harbor found herself asking. "Me, you, and Dad, I mean. On the boat. With Grandpa or whatever."

Mom nodded, then finally moved her gaze away from Harbor to look out at the lagoon. It wouldn't stay this quiet much longer. Not in the summer. Not with the Badger boys and their loud grandma, Brenda Badger, across the street. Not with seventeen-year-old Jamie Perez and her loud music a few houses down. Not with the boats that would drive up and down the lagoon, and the rest of the Ali-O'Connor family waking up soon.

Harbor wished she was a morning person so she could have more moments like these.

"Your dad never liked the boats as much as I did," Mom said. "But, yeah. We did that a lot, at first, when you were born. In those early days, though, it was mostly just you and me. Not on the boat, I couldn't take you alone, but just, the two of us. Looking out at the water."

The deck door opened, and Good Boy ran out and pushed his head into Mom's lap for pets. Mama followed behind him. Seeing Mama, while talking about the life Harbor was too little to remember, the one where it was just her and her dad and her mom, without Mama, made her blush. Mom also stopped talking and fell quiet, and Harbor wondering if, maybe, Mom was feeling weird about it, too.

Harbor stood so Mama could have her seat.

"You're up early," Mama said, just like Mom, as she came over to wrap an arm around Harbor. Harbor was taller than Mama now. Tall enough that Mama could rest her head on Harbor's shoulder, which made Harbor feel older.

Harbor was starting to feel a little too warm. "I should go shower before everyone else hogs the bathroom."

"Oh, don't. Stay out here with us a little longer," Mom said.

Part of Harbor really wanted to stay. A bigger part of her knew that if she didn't get into the bathroom now, the twins would get up, and Marina and Boom would get up, and Sam would get up, and it'd take forever for her to get a turn. And then, maybe, Sonny would get roped into swimming with Pork and the twins, or Sam would come outside and ask him to hang before Harbor could.

"No, I think I'm gonna go in," Harbor said.

Mom gave her a small smile, and Mama gently squeezed her shoulder before she headed toward the door and straight into the bathroom.

The entire house was awake not even five minutes later, shattering the early peace of the morning. Mama was helping the twins make breakfast, while Good Boy waited at her feet hoping for crumbs, and Sam was outside helping Mom get ready for a fishing trip, and Boom and Marina were lying on the deck playing with some footage Boom had on her phone.

As Harbor emerged from the house for the second time that morning, seagulls flew high above her head, cawing loudly, adding their voices to the morning chaos of Sunrise Lagoon.

After lunch, Harbor and Sonny got the kayak ready and pushed it into the lagoon from the Badgers' dock. Sonny got in first, doing his best to hold the kayak steady so they wouldn't tip over as Harbor climbed in. They each grabbed a paddle, and Sonny pushed off the dock.

They did all this mostly in silence. Not that they needed to talk—Sonny's grandpa had bought the kayaks back when Sonny and Harbor were eight, and they were a well-oiled machine by now. They *always* shared a kayak, while Sonny's brothers and Harbor's siblings all rotated who shared the others. Sonny and Harbor didn't need to talk to know where they were headed, or how fast they should paddle, or when they needed to turn or move to the side to let the big boats go by. They did it all by instinct.

Still, Harbor spent the majority of the time trying to think of *something* to say. "How was baseball camp?" she finally asked when they'd stopped paddling and were bobbing around the lagoon, basking in the sunshine. They watched the bigger boats driving out in the bay, waving at the occasional person speeding by on a Jet Ski.

"It was okay."

"It's funny that you were busy with baseball and I was busy with basketball," Harbor said. "We're both super into sports."

"Actually?" Sonny paused for a moment. "Actually, I don't even know that I like baseball anymore? I feel like I just play because I always do. And my dad likes it? But there's always so many games and practices and I kind of don't want to keep doing it so much."

"Oh," Harbor said.

"Do you ever feel like that? With basketball?"

No. She didn't. "I want to play more actually. I'm joining a summer league, by my dad's house. We have all-day practices and games on the weekends."

"Oh," Sonny said. "That sounds like a lot. I would hate that. Sam said you played on two different teams during the school year, too."

Harbor didn't really know what to say to that.

"I saw your mom and Sam went fishing this morning? Why didn't you go with them?" Sonny asked.

Because I wanted to hang with you, Harbor thought. *Because I missed you and I thought if we hung out things would feel the same again like always.* "I didn't feel like it," she said instead. "I guess maybe I feel about fishing and boats like you do about baseball."

"Really?"

"I guess."

"Does Sam still feel the same about fishing and boats?"

Harbor scowled at him. "Why do you keep bringing up Sam? If you want to know what Sam wants or thinks, you'll have to ask her."

Sonny blushed. "Sorry. Yeah. Okay."

Harbor didn't really want to be kayaking anymore. It was hot. She'd forgotten her sunglasses. It wasn't fun right now. "You want to just head back?"

"Yes," Sonny said, a little too quickly for Harbor's liking. "Let's go back."

CHAPTER FIVE

For a house that was too small, it was still impossible to find anything. Harbor had spent all that morning looking for the duffel bag she wanted to bring to her dad's house. "Mom! I can't find my bag!"

"Did you check the hall closet?"

"Yes!"

"Your closet?"

"Yes!"

"Well, I don't know, Harbor, keep better track of your things!"

Harbor wanted to scream. The reason she couldn't keep track of her things was because they had one closet for three of them, and there was so much stuff in it already that they always had to find other places for storage. She couldn't keep track of her things because they could be anywhere, because that was what happened when you had four siblings and two moms and one giant dog and one *way too small house*!

She didn't even realize she was saying all of that out loud until Cordelia appeared beside her. "I like our house. I like that I can say something loudly in one room and everyone can hear me in all the others."

"Cordelia, you could say something up the street and we all would still be able to hear you," Harbor said.

"Also, I think your bag is in our closet."

Harbor practically growled at Cordelia for waiting so long to tell her. She got up from where she was looking under her bed and headed for the twins' bedroom. Their room felt so *spacious* sometimes, since only two of them had to share.

She yanked open their closet, where she did, indeed, find her bag on the floor. "Thank god," she said, lifting it up and turning around to find Cordelia and Lir. They were staring at her. "What?" Harbor snapped.

"Well, we were kind of using your bag," Cordelia said.

Lir anxiously looked over at her. "Well, Cordelia was. I . . . didn't really take part in this one."

Harbor narrowed her eyes. "Take part in what?"

"At the beginning of the school year I wanted to see how quickly my school lunch would get moldy in different places," Cordelia said. She started counting off her fingers. "I put one on the back porch and one in the crab trap and one in your bag in our closet. Only, I guess I forgot about the one in the closet, in your bag, until, well, you started looking for it."

Harbor dropped the bag. It was only then she noticed there were ants crawling all over it.

Lir, seeing the bugs, started panicking. "Oh no, oh no, get it out of our room!"

Harbor took a deep, deep breath before screaming, "*MOOOOOOOOOOM!*"

After all was said and done, Mama let Harbor borrow one of her big beach bags.

"Cordelia is too old to be doing these things," Harbor said as Mama handed her the bag. "It's not cute anymore!"

"Let *us* worry about Cordelia," Mama replied.

"Then worry about her!"

"Take a deep breath, Harbor, and come hug me goodbye before you leave."

By the time Harbor had packed and their moms had lectured Cordelia *and* cleaned their closet with disinfectant and ant spray (and Mom threw Harbor's bag outside to "deal with later," whatever that meant), they were running late. This wasn't unusual. The Ali-O'Connors weren't known for being prompt. There were too many moving pieces, too many things that could go wrong in any given minute that could set them back by five minutes or ten minutes or a half hour.

Harbor hated being late. She hated showing up to basketball practice late, she hated when her moms were late to pick her up from somewhere, and she hated that it was almost always because someone else in her family needed something in that moment more than she did.

Because they were running so late, Mom had to take Sam with them on the drive to her dad's. It was the day Sam visited her grandma where she lived in a nursing home, which was about halfway between home and Harbor's dad. Sam visited her grandma now once a month. Sam used to live with her grandma, who was now too sick now to take care of her, before becoming part of the Ali-O'Connor family. Harbor considered it a consolation prize that she wasn't the only one who fell victim to the chaos of being late this time, that Sam was stuck in the car for longer than should have been necessary.

Still, it wasn't the most welcomed company. Sam and Harbor may have been closest in age—they were only four months apart, in the same grade and classes in school and everything—but they definitely weren't *close*. They sat on either side of the backseat of the car, staring out their respective windows, ignoring each other. It would almost be nice, really, the quiet, if Mom didn't spend the *entire* drive talking loudly on the Bluetooth with a client from Koch's Marina. He needed his motor fixed and couldn't hear a thing, so there was a lot of raised voices and repeating.

It didn't help that Sam seemed super interested in the conversation, like she wanted to learn how to deal with clients and fix boats. Sam wanted to learn to fix boats just like Mom.

Harbor used to want that, too.

She hadn't yet told anyone except for Sonny.

Finally, Mom settled the issue and hung up just as they were turning down the street for Harbor's dad's town house. Mom pulled into the driveway and parked the car, hesitating for a moment. Sometimes Mom would walk Harbor inside. Sometimes she wouldn't. Harbor had yet to figure out how to predict which way it would go.

"You have everything you need for basketball this weekend? I didn't even have time to make sure. You have your sneakers? Your practice clothes?"

"Yeah," Harbor said, holding up the beach bag, desperately hoping her dad had a gym bag or backpack or something better she could swap it for.

"I'll pick you up either Sunday night or Monday. I'll call your dad tomorrow to figure it out," Mom said.

The front door opened, and everyone looked up to see Harbor's dad standing on his front porch. Mom turned the car off and opened her door, obviously having made her decision. Mom came over to Harbor's side of the car to take the beach bag, though Harbor didn't really need any help. Sam stayed in the car, offering Harbor a small smile, while Mom wrapped an arm around Harbor and led her up to her dad's door.

"Hey, kid," he said with a smile.

"Hi, Dad."

"Hey," he said with less of a smile to Harbor's mom.

It wasn't that they didn't get along. All things considered they were plenty friendly to each other. Harbor hadn't seen a big fight between them in a long time, at least. Still, she was only a baby when they separated, and she couldn't imagine them ever being in love and married and happy together.

Mom noticed Harbor's dad eyeing the beach bag filled with Harbor's clothes and basketball sneakers. "We had a mishap with Harbor's bag."

"Of course you did," Harbor's dad said.

"It's fine," Harbor said, deflecting. She decided to lie, just so that they could all move on from it. "I left a gym bag here a while ago I can use for practice."

Her dad didn't need to know she hated having to use Mama's beach bag.

"Okay, come give me a hug," Mom said, turning away from Harbor's dad to pull Harbor into her. Harbor wasn't a hugger, like the twins. She didn't like to hover closely to her moms like Marina sometimes did. She didn't need a hug or a kiss or to hold hands like Sam sometimes did. Her moms never made Harbor hug anyone if she said she didn't want to. Most of the time, she didn't want to.

She let her mom hug her now, anyway.

"Let me know how practice goes. I'll call you tomorrow," Mom said, and the hug was over, and she was talking about pick-up logistics with Harbor's dad, and then she was waving as she walked back down the driveway and climbed into the car where Sam was waiting.

And then it was just Harbor and her dad.

"You hungry?" her dad said. "We can order something. You like pizza, right? Or we've got this excellent Chinese takeout place around the corner. What're you in the mood for?"

"Oh," Harbor said, as he led her in through the front door. "What do you want?"

"You can pick, whatever you want," he said. "You want to go toss your bag into your room and I'll show you all the menus I've got stashed somewhere?"

"Okay. Cool."

Harbor's room at her dad's wasn't really *her* room. It was a guestroom. It had a bed, with a plain blue comforter, and an empty wooden dresser she could use if she wanted. Usually she just kept her clothes in her bag—she never was at her dad's long enough to want to fully settle in. The walls were bare. She put beach bag on the floor, took off her sneakers, placed them against the wall, closed her eyes, and took a deep breath. It wasn't her room.

But she was the only one who ever used it, and she liked how *empty* it was.

Harbor decided on Chinese food for dinner because they never ate it at home. The twins were picky, and Mom said it bothered her stomach, but Harbor really loved lo mein and egg rolls. They ate the food at her dad's coffee table in the living room and looked for something to watch on TV. Harbor chose *Jaws*, which Harbor's moms never let her watch (probably with good reason, since they lived on the water). Harbor wasn't afraid of sharks, though. And her dad quoted half the movie, which made Harbor laugh.

"You know, some of the inspiration for this movie is based off real shark attacks in Matawan, right here in Jersey. Wild, right?"

Oh, Marina would *not* like knowing that fact. But Marina was not here. "No way. Really? When?"

"A long time ago, like early 1900s I think, so you don't need to worry."

"I'm not worried," Harbor said.

"The last thing I need is for your mom to get mad at me for making you afraid of her beloved ocean," her dad said.

"I'm not afraid," Harbor said. "I like this movie and I like the water."

Her dad softly laughed. "Yeah. Your mom raised a little fish, I know. Can't compete all the way up here without the water nice and close, can I?"

Her dad's house was too far north in New Jersey to be by the water. He had to drive south to get to the beach, like the other tourists who flocked to the shore in the summers. There were tall, thick trees behind his town house. No seagulls, no crabs, but sometimes he'd see deer, instead. His town house also had an actual backyard, with grass, where Harbor used to kick a soccer ball around. She used to run around that yard when she was younger. She wasn't allowed to run out back at home.

"That's okay," Harbor said. "I like it here."

"Good," her dad said, and he seemed to relax even more back into the sofa. He bumped her shoulder with his. "That makes me really happy. I like this, watching movies with you. It feels too quiet here sometimes without you."

Harbor really liked the quiet of his home.

After the movie, Harbor brushed her teeth, changed into her pajamas, and climbed into bed—all without having to rush, or worry about someone else needing to pee, or wait for everyone else to get settled before she could turn the light off.

She fell asleep quickly in the quiet of her dad's house.

CHAPTER SIX

Harbor showed up to basketball practice on time. In fact, they were fifteen minutes early. Harbor was able to switch her regular sneakers for her basketball ones without rushing to tie them, which meant they'd probably stay tied all practice. Which was good because, lately, Harbor tended to trip over her own feet without any added obstacles.

But she wasn't as well rested as she thought she'd be. Without Marina's sound machine, she could hear everything. Every creak of the town house, every time the air conditioning kicked on. She heard her dad's alarm clock through the wall before he came to wake her up. It was fine, though. She *liked* that it was quiet enough in the bedroom, in the house, to hear everything. And, anyway, Harbor assumed the real reason she kept waking up was because of how nervous she was about her new basketball team.

Her dad was excited. "I knew Dawn from back when I used to play. She's really talented, she's always been. I think you'll like her."

Harbor's mom had been the one to give her a love of the ocean, but it was her dad who taught her to love basketball. He'd played all through high school and would have played in college, too, if a knee injury hadn't stopped him.

Harbor wasn't necessarily nervous about her new coach. Sure, she wanted to impress Coach Dawn, but she was mostly nervous about meeting all her new teammates. Harbor didn't think she was great at meeting new people. But basketball was a team sport, which meant she had to be a team player, which meant she had to be friendly with her teammates.

Even if that filled her stomach with what felt like a bunch of killifish swimming around too quickly for her liking.

She sat on one of the chairs lined up along the side of the court, waiting for Coach Dawn to begin practice. Harbor's dad had left, but Coach Dawn was chatting with a couple other parents. Some of the girls on the team were tying their sneakers, and a couple were grabbing basketballs to start shooting around. Harbor knew that was what she should be doing, too—coaches liked when their players didn't need to be told what to do or when to start practicing.

Harbor was pretty observant when it came to basketball. She watched enough games and played enough of them, too. So she'd easily spotted the girl who had to be their point guard. She was a Black girl with shaved hair and was the shortest on the team—which the point guard usually was—and Harbor could already tell she had the best ball control out of everyone. Not only that, her eyes moved around the court, constantly aware, even though they hadn't officially started practice yet. That was the point guard's job. To see the whole court and be the floor general.

She passed the ball to a girl shorter than Harbor. (It seemed as though almost everyone on the team was shorter than Harbor—but they were all still taller than Sam, because basketball players tended to be big even when small.) This girl was white with thick brown hair pulled back in a ponytail that waved behind her as she ran to the basket to make an easy layup.

Harbor knew she should go introduce herself to them, and to the other girls on the court. But she couldn't bring herself to move quite yet.

"Hi."

Harbor startled at the sound and looked up—and then looked *up*. This girl was even taller than she was. Her long hair was pulled into a ponytail, the tips dyed a light blue that emphasized the way one side of her head was shaved. She had a basketball hoisted onto her hip, and her sneakers were the brightest neon green Harbor had ever seen. She had tape all along the cartilage of her ear, which probably meant she had piercings she didn't want to take out for practice but wasn't allowed to leave uncovered while playing.

Harbor suddenly realized she'd been staring without saying anything. "Oh. Hi."

"You're the only other tall girl here," her teammate said. Her voice was so soft Harbor had to lean in to hear her over the bounce of the practice balls.

"I was just noticing that," Harbor said.

"I'm Quinn. I don't think I've seen you around before. Not that I've memorized every kid I play basketball against, but, well, Dawn's my aunt so I usually know all her players, and . . ." She paused, blushing as her shoulders scrunched up by her ears. Her voice was even softer when she said, "Sorry. I'm rambling."

"That's okay. My sister rambles. You've got nothing on her," Harbor said. "I'm Harbor. I usually play down south Jersey. Your aunt is friends with my dad, who lives here."

Harbor paused, also blushing a little. She didn't really mind at all that her dad and her mom were divorced, or that she had an entire family separate from her dad, or that she had two moms. It was just, sometimes, exhausting to explain, to answer questions. All the Ali-O'Connors had their own ways of dealing with questions, but Harbor mostly wished other people would mind their own business.

But Quinn didn't ask any questions. "Cool. I live with my aunt, so I can play up here, too."

Harbor didn't ask any questions, either. "Cool."

"Do you want to maybe shoot around while we wait for practice to start? Might be fun to try and block each other, since, you know, we're the tall ones," Quinn said.

Harbor liked the sound of that, for once. It wasn't so bad being one of the tall ones when she had someone to share that with. "Yeah. Sounds good."

Harbor stood up, holding out her hands. Quinn passed her the basketball.

The rest of the weekend was all basketball all the time. Harbor learned that the shorter Black girl was indeed the point guard. Her name was Camryn, and she was already practicing with Olympic training camps. The girl with the thick brown hair was a shooting guard named Fiona, whose dad was an assistant coach for the Memphis Grizzlies, so her entire house lived and breathed basketball.

A bunch of the girls knew one another from various ranked travel teams. Some of them were already talking about scouts watching them play—for high school *and* for college.

They were all very serious about basketball.

Harbor was serious, too. But she'd mostly played on her school team and in her driveway when her mom didn't have a boat hitched on a trailer, and except for Marina, sometimes, no one was interested in watching basketball games with her.

But Harbor never quite knew what to say to the other girls when they weren't playing—especially since Quinn, the one girl she'd come closest to befriending also didn't seem to want to talk. That was fine, though. Because it didn't matter once practice started.

Practice was the same as any team Harbor had ever played on. Harbor wasn't the best at dribbling up and down the court these days—her newly giant feet tended to get in the way—but when it came to shooting around the paint, she didn't miss.

One of the taller girls, a redhead named Geena, whooped loudly as Harbor made a three-pointer. "Coach Dawn, you found us a sharpshooter!"

Harbor tried not to smile at the praise, but when she caught Quinn's eye and Quinn grinned widely at her, Harbor couldn't help but return it.

"Nice shot earlier," Quinn said quietly during the next water break.

"If Quinn is actually talking enough to give you a compliment, you know she means it," Camryn said. "I'm still trying to get her to say 'I'm open' loud enough so I can hear her when I'm looking for someone to pass to."

Quinn shrugged, smile still on her face, which let Harbor know that the teasing wasn't meant to be mean.

"I'll be loud enough for the both of us," Harbor said. "You have to be pretty loud in my family to survive."

"I'll hold you to that, sharpshooter," Camryn replied.

Mom picked Harbor up after dinner on Sunday. Harbor would have preferred she come get her the next morning, but Mom had needed to transport a boat from the marina to its owner who lived only twenty minutes away from Harbor's dad.

Pick up was always a little easier than drop off. Mom texted she was there, Harbor said goodbye to her dad, grabbed her things, walked out the door, and hopped in the car. Nice and easy, no awkward small talk between her parents. "Hey, you. I missed you," Mom said, leaning over to give Harbor a big wet kiss on the side of her head.

"Mom, ew," she said, wiping it off.

"Tell me about your new team. How was your weekend?"

Harbor thought carefully about her answer. She thought about getting Chinese food for dinner (and getting to eat the leftovers for lunch before they were all gone) and the big quiet bedroom that wasn't hers but also was *only* hers. She thought about how Coach Dawn corrected her stance so she didn't trip over her feet as much and the way Camryn and Fiona kept calling her sharpshooter. She thought about Quinn being even taller than she was, and how nice it was to play with someone who could block her shots. She thought about the quiet way Quinn would say she was open that wasn't really helpful but that made Harbor smile anyway.

She also thought about watching movies with her dad and how much he seemed to like her company.

"It was good," Harbor said.

"Happy to be headed home to the family for the week?"

"Yeah," Harbor said, because she knew that was what Mom wanted her to say.

The air changed the closer they got to home. It was cooler, breezier by the water, despite the heat and the humidity. The sky filled with seagulls and the trees got thinner and thinner until there was nothing but yellow-green marshland and the blue of the bay. Harbor liked that shift—she liked that it felt like she was crossing a border between her parents' houses that transported her from one world to another.

When they got to their street, Harbor *did* really feel happy to be home. As Mom pulled into the driveway, Harbor spotted the ospreys in their nests and she squinted, trying to count the baby birds in the nest. "I think there are three this year," she said.

"What?" Mom asked.

Harbor pointed to the nest. It was on top of a big wooden pole out in the marshlands that was built for the ospreys to make their homes in. "Baby ospreys. I think there are three."

She and Mom leaned against the car, the beach bag hung over Harbor's shoulder, and they watched the ospreys. Mom wrapped an arm around Harbor, squeezing her close. "I missed you," she said for the second time. "Let's go inside."

She followed Mom to the front door.

The peace shattered almost immediately.

As soon as they opened the door, the sounds of Cordelia's sobs were the only thing that Harbor could hear. She was sitting on the counter, crying big wet tears. Mama stood in front of her, gently dabbing Neosporin on her knee. Beside them, Lir was crying, too.

"What happened?" Mom said as Good Boy came charging down the hall at the sound of her voice.

Good Boy barked and headbutted Harbor's chest, and then Mom's, and then Harbor's again, excited his people were back home. Harbor tried to pet him, but he was too worked up to stay still, his long, heavy tail whipping back and forth, which Harbor tried, unsuccessfully, to dodge.

"The . . . seagull . . . took . . . my . . . ice cream," Lir said between sobs.

"It startled them, and Cordelia fell onto the rocks," Mama explained, raising her voice so Mom could hear her over the twins.

Harbor pushed past Good Boy, trying to get to her bedroom so she could put down the heavy beach bag. When she got there, Boom, of course, was over. She and Marina were sprawled out on the beds—Marina's and Harbor's—with notebook paper spread out all around them. "What are you doing?" Harbor snapped.

"Hang on, we'll be done in a bit," Marina responded.

"Marina's helping me storyboard for my next film," Boom explained.

"Why are you doing it on my bed?" Harbor asked.

"You weren't here," Marina said simply, before she and Boom got back to their work, completely ignoring Harbor's presence once again.

Harbor let the beach bag fall heavy and hard onto the bedroom floor before stomping back out to her moms to tell them to make Boom go home. It was getting late, anyway, and she wanted her bed, and she wanted to put her things away, and she wanted someone to acknowledge she was home now.

"Mom—" she started, but then the back door slammed open, which had Mom yelling "Don't slam that door!" and Sam and Sonny saying, "Sorry!" at the same time. That was when Harbor noticed that the two of them, Sonny and Sam, were in their bathing suits, hair wet, wrapped up in beach towels. They'd been hanging out in the lagoon without her.

Sam noticed Harbor before Sonny. "Oh. You're home."

Harbor swallowed. It went down her throat hard. "Yeah. I'm home."

"Can one of you please get me a Band-Aid?" Mama said.

The twins kept crying.

Boom was still in Harbor's bedroom.

Harbor turned on her heel and headed to the bathroom. Good Boy tried to follow her in, but she shut the door, keeping him out, and turned on the faucet to drown out the sound of everyone else in the house.

She sat on the closed toilet lid with her eyes closed, taking one long moment to be alone.

CHAPTER SEVEN

All the Ali-O'Connor siblings approached reading much differently. Cordelia and Lir, though they had been very good at reading on their own from a young age, still preferred to be read to by one or both of their moms. Marina blew through books like they were nothing; she was always the first one to get her summer reading done, which was exceptionally frustrating for both Harbor and Sam.

Sam was the slowest. She had the hardest time reading, and though their moms had been working with her—and she had extra help during the school year—she still wasn't as good as her siblings. Though, luckily for Sam, she wasn't usually the last one to finish her summer reading. Harbor tended to procrastinate until the last second. It wasn't that she didn't like reading, it was just that most of the time she didn't like the books she was assigned.

Their moms tried to get everyone to start their reading early in the summer so they weren't scrambling at the last minute, and they were somewhat successful most summers. That was why after the chaos of the seagull, and Sonny and Boom had gone home, Mom was currently with the twins, taking turns reading aloud from *Charlotte's Web*. Marina was almost finished reading *The Tale of Despereaux*, Sam was chewing on her lip as she slowly flipped through the pages of *Brown Girl Dreaming*, and Harbor was pretending to read *The War That Saved My Life*. (She and Sam, who were in the same grade, would swap when they both finished, whenever that would be.)

The book wasn't bad—it was actually pretty good—but Harbor was mostly just enjoying that while everyone was reading, no one was *talking*. Besides, well, Mom and the twins, but Harbor even enjoyed that a little, the sound of their voices as they slowly read about Wilbur the pig. She put her book down on her chest just to listen to them for a little while.

There was a soft knock on their bedroom door, and Marina, Sam, and Harbor all picked their heads up to see Mama standing on the threshold. She winked at the three of them. "You can all keep reading," she said, before crossing the room to Harbor's bed. Harbor shifted over, making room, as Mama climbed in to lay beside her.

"Sorry I was busy when you got home," Mama said quietly. Harbor shrugged. "It's fine."

"I'd love to hear all about your new basketball team," Mama said.

"It's good. Coach Dawn is cool. She showed me how to fix my footwork," Harbor said. "And her niece is on my team. Her name is Quinn. She's taller than I am, and we practiced together. It was nice. I feel like I always play against girls who are shorter than me. And Quinn was cool. It was cool."

"Cool," Mama said with another wink.

"How much do I need to read tonight?" Sam asked Mama from her bed.

"How much have you read?" Mama asked.

"Twenty-three pages," Sam said.

"Can you get to twenty-five tonight?"

"Okay."

It got quiet again as Sam settled back into the book. Harbor thought that maybe Mama would leave, but she didn't yet. Harbor picked the book up off her chest and started skimming the pages, and Mama still didn't leave.

"How was it at your dad's?" Mama said after a moment.

"Good."

Mama started playing with Harbor's hair. "You can talk to me about anything. You know that, right? About basketball or your dad's or anything."

"I know," Harbor said. "My dad's was good. We ordered takeout every night. He let me watch *Jaws*. I have my own room." Harbor knew she was being a little bit of a brat—she was ticking off all the things she wasn't allowed to do or couldn't have here—but she did it anyway. It was like something had cracked open in her chest and the words kept pouring out. "I like it. It's nice."

"You watched *Jaws*?" Marina said. "I will never *ever* watch *Jaws*."

"That's probably for the best," Mama said.

"I wasn't scared," Harbor said. "It was fun. Dad had fun, with me…" Harbor's voice trailed off. She glanced over at Mama, who was listening closely, and suddenly Harbor, without knowing why, kind of felt like she wanted to cry. She shifted a little closer to Mama. She didn't want to talk about her dad anymore. Not with Mama, who wasn't a piece of that part of Harbor's life.

When she was little, she used to wonder what it would be like if Mom and her dad had never split up. But that would mean no Mama, and that was weird to wonder about at all. "Mama?" Harbor said, even though Mama was already listening, just because she wanted to say it out loud. "Can we read together for a little bit?"

Her cheeks grew warm after she asked it, feeling a little babyish.

But Mama said, "Of course we can." She picked up the book and started from where Harbor left off.

Mom took Sam and Cordelia fishing later that week. Harbor had, again, declined. Unlike Marina, who was picky about when she went on the boats because they made her nervous, Harbor was picky because, lately, she just didn't feel like going fishing anymore.

Mom asked her about twelve times if she was sure. Harbor *was* sure. With Sam on the boat, and Marina at Boom's house, Harbor could hang at home by herself. Mama was out back watching Lir and Pork Badger swim in the lagoon, and Harbor sat on the floor in the living room, scratching Good Boy's ears, deciding what she should do with her delightful free time.

There was a knock on the front door, which set Good Boy into hysterics. He jumped off Harbor's lap, knocking her over and barking his head off.

Harbor sighed as she swung the door open, revealing Sonny Badger on the other side, holding tight to Good Boy's collar so he wouldn't make a run for it or jump on top of Sonny. "Sam's not home," Harbor snapped, a little rudely.

"Do you want to come crabbing?" Sonny said, not missing a beat. He was, at least, used to Harbor's moods. "My grandma is really mad at my grandpa. Because he bought chicken at the store that went bad before we used it? And she didn't know? But anyway, he said we could have it to go crabbing. If you want?"

Sonny thrust a package of raw chicken legs at Harbor.

She shoved the chicken away from her face, but she was smiling. This was what summer was supposed to be. Her and

Sonny and Sunrise Lagoon. "Let me grab my flip flops and tell Mama. I'll meet you out front."

Sonny and Harbor, with the chicken legs and the wire string that Harbor had taken from Mom's shed and a bucket Sonny had borrowed from his grandpa, made their way up the road to the marshlands that overlooked the bay. They stood up on the wooden planks that surrounded the marshland from the main road, using the pillars to steady themselves, and they tied the string around one chicken leg each. Then they slowly lowered the bait into the bay.

Mom had taught Harbor how to crab when she was so little Harbor couldn't even remember learning. Sonny's grandpa had done the same with the Badger brothers. They stood side by side, waiting. Eventually, they hoped, one or both of them would feel a tug as a crab nibbled at the chicken, and they would slowly, *slowly*, start lifting the string.

They didn't realize they had forgotten to bring a net until Mr. Martin, their neighbor from a couple houses down, brought them one. "Saw you two out here without a net. Here, use mine. It's the best net for crabbing, anyway. And I should know. I'm the best crabber on Sunrise Lagoon," Mr. Martin said.

"Don't let my mom hear you say that," Harbor replied.

"Please. Who do you think taught her when she was just a tadpole, huh?" Mr. Martin said. He stood with them for a little bit, until Mr. Harris, another neighbor—and Mr. Martin's best friend—came jogging over, too. He was carrying a small crab trap.

"Thought you two might want to use it," Mr. Harris said. "It's my older one, so I barely use it anymore. You can keep it tied up here if you want."

"Thanks, Mr. Harris," Sonny said, and then he and Mr. Harris got the trap ready. Sonny put the chicken leg inside the wire trap, and Mr. Harris tied it onto one of the planks. Mr. Martin helped them hoist it over the side, and the four of them watched it sink into the water.

"Well, good luck to you both!" Mr. Martin said, and he and Mr. Harris made their way back to Mr. Martin's house.

"Oh, I think I got one," Sonny said soon after. He slowly started pulling up his string, and Harbor grabbed the net, ready to scoop up a crab.

But there was nothing on the string. "Oh. I thought I felt something?"

"Maybe it let go," Harbor said.

He dropped the string back into the water.

The sun was strong, and Harbor wiped the hair back from her forehead where it was clinging. Sonny's shoulder was pressed against hers. She wanted to catch a good amount of crabs. If they did, she could ask Sonny if he'd want to come over and make something with them, crab dip maybe, if he still liked to cook as much as he did last summer. She hoped he did. She hoped a whole school year apart didn't entire change who Sonny was.

She opened her mouth to ask if he still wanted to be a chef, if he would cook something with the crabs that they caught, but Sonny spoke first. "I like Sam, Harbor," he said quickly and a little too loud.

It took her by surprise. "Oh. I know? I mean, I get that you guys hang out when I'm not around. It's fine. She's your friend, too, I get it."

Sonny's shoulders slumped, his face turned bright pink. "No. I mean, yeah? I mean. Harbor, I *like* Sam. I don't know if she likes me, too? Maybe she doesn't? But I like Sam, and I thought you should know?"

Harbor couldn't breathe.

Harbor should have seen this coming.

Of course Sonny liked Sam. He always wanted to hang out with Sam, and he always asked about Sam, and why didn't she realize this sooner?

"Oh," Harbor said.

"Is that weird for you?"

Yes. "Why?"

"Because she's your sister, and I—"

"No, I mean . . . why *Sam*," Harbor said through a clenched jaw.

"Oh. I don't know? She's really nice and really pretty and—"

"Why not *me*, Sonny?"

The question startled Sonny so much, he let go of his string. The chicken leg quickly submerged deep into the water. They watched it sink lower and lower, down to the bottom of the bay, where the crabs would eat it without having to worry about being caught in a trap.

"Do you like *me* like that?" Sonny asked. His voice was a little high and squeaky, and he cringed a little as he asked it.

"No!" Harbor practically shouted. She really, really didn't like Sonny that way at all. "That's not the point!"

"Then what—"

"Does she like you?"

"I don't know!"

"Why are you telling me this?"

"Because you're my friend?" Sonny said. "I mean, you are! You're my *best* friend! So I thought I could . . . I don't know why you're so upset!"

Was this why everything with Sonny felt differently this summer? Was it because he liked Sam? He had *Sam*, so Harbor didn't matter anymore?

She was clenching her teeth harder and harder, because if she didn't, she would cry. She refused to let Sonny Badger make her cry.

She thrust the string she was holding into Sonny's hand, and he grabbed it tight before her chicken leg fell into the water, too. "You can finish crabbing. I don't feel like it anymore," Harbor said.

She turned to walk home, leaving Sonny behind.

CHAPTER EIGHT

The Fourth of July fell on a Sunday this summer. That meant Harbor was, for the first time in her entire life, going to be celebrating at her dad's house instead of on the boat with the rest of the Ali-O'Connors.

It was what they did every year. Mom would take the family, along with the Badger brothers, on Mom's biggest boat, the *Sunrise Princess*. They'd sail out to Tices Shoal, a shallow area along the Barnegat Bay where everyone would anchor their boats and party. When the sun went down, all of Sunrise Lagoon would lay back and watch the fireworks. Even Marina, who'd missed the Fourth of July last year because of a new-found fear of boats, said she would be going this year.

Harbor's first basketball game with her new team that Saturday, and they had practice on Sunday. Her dad said he'd take her to the local fireworks that evening, if she wanted. He sounded excited about it.

Mom was *not* excited about it. "I can come get you Sunday morning."

"I have practice," Harbor said. "You wouldn't be able to get me and get us back in time, and I don't want to leave early. I *can't* leave early! It would look bad!"

"It won't be the same without you," Mom said. She sounded so small, and Harbor hated it.

"There are plenty of fun summer traditions we'll make sure Harbor is home for," Mama said. Harbor shot her a grateful look. "It's just one Fourth of July."

It was *just* one Fourth of July.

That was what Harbor kept telling herself when she arrived at her dad's for the weekend. It was easy enough to ignore the holiday when she had basketball to focus on all day Saturday. Particularly since that night was her first game with her new team, and she was nervous. Her moms had asked (and asked and asked) if it was okay that they wouldn't be able to go—there would be so much traffic on a holiday weekend, and Mom had to work at the marina all day—but Harbor had shrugged them off. At least she wouldn't have to worry about her family making a ruckus in the stands.

She sat on the bench while the bleachers filled up with her teammates' friends and family, tying and retying her sneakers.

A shadow covered her, and she looked up to see Quinn standing there. "Need help?" Quinn said quietly, motioning to Harbor's sneakers.

Harbor blushed. "Oh, no. I mean, I can tie my shoes."

Quinn shifted her weight from one foot to the other and back again, rocking from side to side. "You'll do great, Harbor. You killed it in practice today."

"Thanks," Harbor said, glancing away. Quinn never said much—she was the anti-Cordelia. During practice, Quinn did as she was coached, nodding silently and confidently, and just played the game. But that meant Coach Dawn often told Quinn she had to communicate better with her teammates during play.

So did Camryn, who would hold a hand to her ear every time Quinn called for the ball. "Did someone say something?"

But being so quiet meant that when Quinn did speak up, Harbor knew she was serious.

Like when Harbor stole the ball from Geena during a practice scrimmage and broke away, running down the court to make a layup, Quinn let out a louder-than-usual *whoop!*

Now, Coach Dawn came to stand next to Quinn and put a hand on her shoulder. It made Harbor wonder how Dawn was Quinn's aunt—Dawn was Black, Quinn was white, for starters—but Harbor didn't ask. Maybe Quinn was adopted, maybe she wasn't. Maybe Quinn would want to tell Harbor someday, but until then, Harbor hated being asked those questions, so she wouldn't impose them on Quinn, either.

"You two ready? Quinn, I'm starting you at the five today. Harbor, be ready to sub in," Coach Dawn said.

Harbor froze in the middle of retying her sneaker. She wasn't starting? She couldn't remember the last time she hadn't started. "Um, Coach Dawn?" she said. "I can play the four, too. I don't need to play center." She had been practicing in both positions.

"Everyone has a role, Harbor. Your job is to understand what that is, whether you're starting or coming off the bench," Coach Dawn said.

It wasn't exactly what Harbor was hoping to hear.

The game started without her. Harbor tried not to look at her dad in the crowd. At least the rest of her family wasn't there, cheering obnoxiously loud while she sat on the bench. She didn't play the *entire* first quarter.

But then she went in for the second, and she absolutely rocked it. She almost tripped during a break away, but she planted her feet just like Coach Dawn taught her and passed the ball over everyone's heads to Fiona, who made an easy basket. It was a great pass, a great assist, and Harbor turned to look for her family.

And then caught sight of her dad and remembered the rest of her family wasn't there to shout for her. "Atta girl, Harbor!" he said when he caught her eye.

She was pulled out before the end of the second quarter and didn't play the third, either, but when she went in the fourth and final, she hit the ground running again. Her team was winning by eleven points, most of them scored by Quinn. Harbor found that, as she watched Quinn play, she got less and less upset that Quinn had started over her. Quinn was good. Quinn was *great*.

Harbor really liked watching her play.

Camryn passed Harbor the ball, and when she went to shoot, the other team fouled her. That meant free throws.

Harbor always got nervous taking free throws.

She could make them nonstop in her driveway.

She could make them no problem at practice.

But when everyone in the auditorium was quiet, and staring at *her*, well, she wasn't so great at them.

She bounced the ball a couple times before lining up the shot. The room was quiet. Really, really quiet.

Too quiet.

Cordelia isn't here to shout for you. Neither is Mom.

You wanted this.

I still wish Mom was here.

Just focus and take the shot.

"You've got this, sharpshooter," Camryn said.

"Yeah, come on, line it up, Harbor," Geena added.

And then, a small voice from the bench that Harbor heard loud and clear, "Let's go, Harbor!"

Harbor turned to meet Quinn's eyes. Quinn gave her a thumbs-up.

Harbor breathed in deeply and took the shot.

Harbor made both of her free throws *and* two others *and* her team won *and* her dad was so proud of her he took her out for ice cream immediately afterward. She called Mom on the drive to the ice cream parlor, but she only got to talk to Mom for about thirty seconds before Cordelia stole the phone, and then she got passed to Lir, who passed it to Mama, who passed it to Sam, who passed it to Marina, who promptly hung up on her.

Harbor's dad let her get a large ice cream. She carefully picked her three scoops: mint chocolate chip, regular chocolate, and peanut butter. Her dad got butter pecan, which Harbor promptly sampled and absolutely did not like.

"Hey, so, I was thinking about the Fourth of July tomorrow," her dad said.

Harbor was trying to lick her melting ice cream before it could drip off her cone, but this made her stomach flip, the reminder that she was missing the Fourth of July on the lagoon. "Oh?"

"Dawn asked if we wanted to go to the firework show with them. It's at the high school football field, we bring blankets and, like, snacks and stuff, sort of like a picnic, and everyone spreads out along the field. It's a whole festival-type thing. County fair-style games and stuff. How's that sound?" her dad asked.

"With Coach Dawn?"

"And her niece. She's on your team?"

"Oh. Yeah. Quinn," Harbor said, nodding. "She started in my position."

Her dad nudged her with his shoulder. "You'll earn that spot soon enough. But what do you say? Sound like a good Fourth of July?"

Harbor shrugged. It would be different. But different didn't need to mean bad. At least she would get to hang out with Quinn. "Yeah. Sounds like a plan."

So the following evening, Harbor and her dad met up with Coach Dawn and Quinn at the Paramus High School North Football Field. Harbor was used to the crowds at Tices Shoal, but she was still surprised to see how packed it was. Half of the parking lot was blocked off and filled with tents that had fair games and funnel cakes and 50/50 tables. There was even a Ferris wheel and a giant slide.

"Let's go get a spot on the field before we explore," Coach Dawn said.

Quinn leaned in close to Harbor, her voice too quiet, to say, "Otherwise it's impossible to get a good spot."

Someone bumped into Quinn, and she quickly grabbed Harbor's hand so they wouldn't be separated. "Sorry," she whispered.

"It's okay," Harbor said. She glanced down at their hands. She thought she was too old to hold someone's hands— Cordelia even fought against holding Mama's these days—but this felt different, so she didn't let go.

She kind of liked it.

The football field was crowded, too, full of families with blankets and tailgating chairs. Harbor couldn't help but smile. This could be *just* as good as the celebration at home. Coach Dawn found a spot and Harbor's dad spread out a large, old New York Giants blanket next to Coach Dawn's even larger New York Liberty blanket. Harbor and Quinn jumped onto the Liberty blanket and Harbor's dad pretended to be offended, which made everyone laugh.

Quinn talked Coach Dawn into letting her buy a funnel cake, so Harbor followed Quinn to the stand closest to where her dad and Coach Dawn were sitting. The line wasn't that long, but as they stood there, neither one of them said anything. Harbor figured Quinn wasn't talking because Quinn wasn't a talker. Still, it felt weird to just stand there in silence.

But Harbor didn't really know what to talk about, either. She didn't know Quinn all that well, even though she liked watching Quinn play basketball and she kind of liked holding Quinn's hand. Harbor, who had been going to the same school since kindergarten, who had been best friends with Sonny for even longer, couldn't remember the last time she made a new friend.

Which made Harbor think about how back home, right now, Sonny was probably on Mom's boat, the boat named after Harbor, *Harbor Me*, with the rest of the Ali-O'Connors. With *Sam*.

"The weather is nice," Harbor suddenly said, and immediately groaned. "Oh my god. I'm sorry. The weather is *not* interesting."

That made Quinn laugh and duck her head a bit. "Sorry. I guess I'm not really good at this."

"At what?"

"When we have basketball parties, sometimes I think the other girls forget I'm there. But it's not because I'm not having fun. I just like to watch and listen more than be part of it all sometimes." The line moved, and they took a step forward. "But I like being part of it here, with you. So far at least."

That made Harbor smile. "I like being part of it here with you so far at least, too."

They got their funnel cake and headed back to their spot, sprawling out together, long limbs covering every inch of the blanket, and got powdered sugar everywhere. Quinn even got some on her nose, and Harbor just kept staring at it instead of telling her. She didn't know why she didn't tell Quinn to wipe it off. She kept smiling at it instead. They didn't talk much, but it was nice. Maybe this was what Quinn meant. Harbor wasn't used to having someone to sit beside her in companionable silence.

They didn't have many silences at home.

When Quinn finally did break that silence, Harbor could barely hear her. "What?"

"Do you have a favorite kind of firework?" Quinn repeated.

Harbor shook her head. "Do you?"

"The ones that look like Kooshes."

"Like what?"

"A Koosh ball!" Quinn's laugh was as quiet as everything else about her, but it made her entire body wiggle when she did. "You know, the little rubber stringy ball thingy!"

"I have no idea what that is," Harbor said, laughing, too.

"I'll point them out," Quinn said.

"Cool."

Quinn finally wiped her nose, and the powdered sugar disappeared. Harbor was kind of disappointed.

"You had a really great game yesterday," Coach Dawn suddenly said as the sun dipped lower and lower in the sky and the football field got even more crowded.

Harbor ducked her head a little at the compliment. And if Coach Dawn thought she was so good, why hadn't she started her?

"I might have to poach you to play for our regular season AAU team. It's competitive, and we travel a bit, but I'd love to get you into a practice and see how you fare with the rest of my players." Coach Dawn flicked Harbor's dad in the ear, in a friendly way. Harbor didn't think she'd ever seen another adult treat her dad that way before. "What do you think, Doug?"

Quinn looked at Harbor with big eyes. "We could play together all year!"

Harbor thought she might want that, too. A chance to prove to Coach Dawn she could be an excellent starter, even compared to Coach Dawn's best players. A chance to keep playing with Quinn.

But she already knew she wouldn't be able to.

"I don't think Harbor's mom would drive her up here for practices after school," Harbor's dad said. "She's only with me on the weekends. And during the school year, she's only here one weekend a month. She's usually with her mom and her mom's wife."

Harbor felt herself blushing, again. She didn't like that her dad never referred to Mama as Harbor's mom, too, and she didn't like that her dad was spilling her entire private life to Coach Dawn and Quinn without asking if she minded.

"Ah, I forgot," Coach Dawn said.

Quinn deflated a bit, too.

"Well, maybe we could work something out?" Harbor said, giving her dad puppy-dog eyes that could rival Good Boy's.

Her dad looked at Harbor carefully before saying, "Maybe."

"Oh! Look! It's starting!" Quinn said, pointing at the sky.

Harbor didn't see anything. And then there was a loud burst, and it was bright and blue—just like the tips of Quinn's hair.

"That's it!" Quinn said, pointing at the next firework that went off, golden in color, with streaks of light that fell slowly down the sky. "That's the Koosh."

Harbor turned to look at Quinn. The colors of the lights danced off Quinn's face. Watching the fireworks was the most animated Harbor had ever seen her. During basketball, Quinn was sturdy and calm, a tall beacon for the rest of the team to look to for guidance. But maybe there were different ways to watch and listen.

Quinn must have noticed Harbor staring because she turned to look back at Harbor, too. "I'm glad you're on the team," Quinn said.

"Me, too," Harbor agreed.

Quinn reached for Harbor's shoulder and pulled her back to lay on the blanket beside her, shoulder to shoulder, as they watched the sky.

It was late when Harbor and her dad got home. "I really liked that," Harbor told him, and she meant it.

"Maybe we could do it again next year?" her dad said, sounding hopeful.

"Maybe," Harbor said.

She started heading for her bedroom when he called after her. "Hey, Harbor?"

Harbor paused and turned to look at him. "Yeah?"

"I really like having you here. It's been fun so far, right?"

"Yeah. Definitely," she said.

"You like your team, right? You're making friends, right?"

"Yeah. I like it a lot."

"Your mom'll be here in the morning, but if we get up early enough, maybe we can go outside and practice shooting around a bit?"

"Yeah, okay."

He fell quiet, and Harbor took that as her cue to start heading to her bedroom.

"Harbor," he said, and she stopped again. She turned to look at him, to wait for whatever it was he wanted to say. "I know there's not a ton of space with all the kids back at your mom's house. And you're older now, you know? If you're serious about basketball . . . and, well, I really like having you here. It's been a long while since we got to spend this kind of time together. We have fun, right?"

He was talking in circles. "Yeah, Dad."

"If you want to play for Dawn's team, during the school year . . . maybe you can," he said. "Maybe you can stay here with me."

Harbor didn't know what to say.

She thought about getting to keep playing with Coach Dawn, and with Quinn. She thought about having her own bedroom. About how nice and quiet her dad's house was. She thought about Marina and Sam and Boom taking up her bedroom, about the twins taking up her moms' attention, about Sonny . . . about Sonny not feeling the same anymore.

About Sunrise Lagoon not feeling the same anymore.

Maybe Harbor wasn't the same anymore, either.

She smiled at her dad, thinking about all the possibilities.

"Yeah. Maybe."

CHAPTER NINE

Harbor wasn't an Ali-O'Connor. Not technically. Not like the rest of her siblings. Harbor's last name was Moore. Once upon a time, Mom was Mrs. Moore, but when Harbor was a baby, that changed. After the divorce, Mom went back to her maiden name, O'Connor. Then she fell in love and married Mama and took her name—Ali—too.

When they adopted Marina as a newborn, she became an Ali-O'Connor. The twins were born Ali-O'Connors. Even Sam, who'd lived with them for four years, had gotten to change her last name to Ali-O'Connor after she was adopted.

But Harbor, unlike Mom, unlike Sam, never got to change her name. They never even asked her if she wanted to.

That was what Harbor couldn't stop thinking about as she played with the homemade mac and cheese Mama had made for dinner. That was, until Boom—who was over for dinner, because of *course* Boom was over for dinner—knocked over her glass of lemonade. In her attempt to grab the glass, and in Lir's attempt to leap across the kitchen and out of the way of the spilling juice, someone knocked into Cordelia's bowl. The bowl landed in Cordelia's lap, mac and cheese spilling onto her pants and then onto the floor, much to Good Boy's delight.

"Oh my stars! Oh my stars! I'm so sorry!" Boom was shouting.

"It's okay, Boom!" Mama said, as she got up to help Cordelia and try and control the mess. Good Boy, too big to actually fit under the table, kept bumping his head on it, nearly knocking over even more glasses of lemonade.

Luckily, everyone was pretty much done with dinner anyway. "Boom, Marina, go take Good Boy for a walk so he's out of our way," Mom said. Sam and Lir quickly gathered the rest of the plates to dump into the sink, and then they, too, disappeared. It left Mama at the sink with Cordelia, taking a damp paper towel to Cordelia's pants, while Mom cleaned her chair, the floor, and the table.

Through it all, Harbor sat quietly. Normally, the ordeal would have had her shouting and annoyed. She just kept playing with her food instead. Watching and listening.

Mom, of course, noticed. "Okay. What's wrong, sweetheart?" she said, abandoning her towel to sit across from Harbor. "You've been quiet all day."

Harbor glanced over at Mama, who was busy cleaning Cordelia's pants, while Cordelia was picking at the leftover mac and cheese.

"Nothing. Well, I mean. Has Dad said anything to you?" Harbor asked.

Now Mom glanced over at Mama, who glanced back. "No . . . why? Did something happen?" Mom asked.

"No. I mean, well. Dad said something. And I thought maybe he'd mention it to you."

"What'd your dad say, Harbor?" Mom asked.

Harbor suddenly felt a little bit like she was in an interrogation.

"Nothing bad or anything. He just, maybe, sort of asked if I wanted to stay with him. Like, during the school year," Harbor quickly said, looking down at her now cold mac and cheese.

"What?" Cordelia asked, sounding completely baffled. "*Why?*"

Mama threw the dirty paper towels away. "Cordelia, go take these off and put your pajamas on. Bring me your dirty clothes, and I'll get them in the wash. Do not leave them on your floor." Cordelia didn't move at first. "Cordelia, now please."

"Coach Dawn said I could play on her AAU team all year. Not just summer camp. But Dad said—"

"Your dad should have had this conversation with me first," Mom said. She sounded kind of angry, and Harbor felt herself tensing up, too.

Mama came to sit at the table now that Cordelia had gone to her room. "We'll talk with your dad about this, okay, Harbor?"

"Yes, we will," Mom muttered under her breath, before saying to Harbor, "You don't need to worry about this, okay? I'll take care of it."

"Oh, okay," Harbor said, feeling a little confused and off-kilter. This wasn't where she thought the conversation would go. "It's just . . . well, I told him maybe. I said maybe I would."

The kitchen got very, very quiet. Mom got very, very still. Then she took a deep breath and said, "It's not your decision to make, Harbor."

Which startled Harbor a little. "Well, why not?"

"Because you're *twelve*. You know what? Why don't you go to your room, Harbor, so Mama and I can talk about this," Mom said, and Harbor knew a dismissal when she heard one. She didn't think it was all that fair. She didn't think her part in this conversation was over.

"Why does *she* get a say in this and I don't?" Harbor said, raising her voice a little as she pointed a finger in Mama's direction.

Mom fixed Harbor with a stern look. "*She* is your mother."

Which made Harbor feel really, really guilty for a moment. "No, I know, that's not what I meant," she said. She couldn't look in Mama's direction. "But he's my *dad!*"

"Harbor—"

"No!" Harbor yelled. "You don't even have room for me here! The three of us are shoved into that bedroom like sardines, I have *zero* privacy. I have an entire room to myself at Dad's! You always drop me off late to basketball practice, you barely notice if I'm here or not because someone is always crying or inviting their friends to sleep over in *my* room, or using *my* things for their science experiments. Dad actually *wants* me there. He has time for me. Why shouldn't he get to spend time with me when you've got a million other kids and I'm too big for this house!"

The front door swung open as Marina and Boom came back in. Good Boy, who hated whenever anyone fought, immediately sensed that something was amiss. He rushed over, whining, looking back and forth between Harbor and Mom.

"What's going on?" Marina asked.

"Go to your room, please," Mama said.

"I work myself to the bone for you, Harbor," Mom said, her voice getting dangerously low. "You have no idea— You know what? I'm not fighting with you, I'm ending this conversation."

"You can't just decide we're done talking!"

"Yes, I can. I can make these decisions, Harbor, because I am your mother. And believe it or not, I know what I'm doing and I know what's best for you!"

Mom stood up, pushing her chair under the table a little too roughly, slamming it down and making Harbor jump. Mom stormed off, down the hall and into her bedroom where she slammed the door shut, too. Harbor watched her with wide eyes, surprised that Mom stormed off before she did, but at least Mom had somewhere to storm off to. That was the point, wasn't it? If Harbor stormed off, there would be Sam or Marina or *someone* in her way.

"Whoa," Boom said. She and Marina were still standing by the front door.

Harbor was relieved that at least Boom wasn't filming them like she always did.

Harbor was breathing a little heavy when she turned to finally look at Mama. Mama looked torn between following Mom and staying with Harbor.

Harbor looked away.

"I'm going to my room," she said, and left Mama standing in the kitchen.

That night, Sam had a nightmare.

When Sam first came to live with the Ali-O'Connors, she had nightmares almost every night. It took a while for Sam to get used to her new home and her new family and to settle the thoughts that made it hard to sleep at night. Her counselor helped with that. So did their moms. Now, she didn't have nightmares often at all.

But sometimes she still did.

It woke Harbor up. Sam tossed and turned a lot during a normal night, but she did it extra when she was having a nightmare. She also mumbled and whimpered, too. Harbor had seen Sam have enough nightmares to know immediately, without even looking at her, what was happening.

Harbor groaned and climbed out of her bed. Marina, with her sound machine basically right next to her head, kept on sleeping undisturbed.

Harbor next to Sam's bed and shook her gently. "Sam," she whispered. "*Sam*," she said a little louder. "Wake up. You're having a bad dream."

Sam startled awake. Her eyes were a little wild before they came into focus. "What?"

"You were having a bad dream, I think?"

"Yeah."

"You okay?"

Sam didn't say anything at first, but then she slowly nodded.

Harbor sighed. "Move over," she said, pushing Sam over a little so she could climb into Sam's small twin-sized bed. They were pressed together from shoulders to toes (well, to mid-calf, because Harbor was longer than Sam). They lay in silence for a few moments, Marina's sound machine whirring in the background, before Harbor said, "Do you . . . want to talk about it, or . . . ?"

"I don't really remember it."

"Okay."

Sam shifted a bit, which made Harbor shift a bit, too.

"It was weird without you there on the Fourth of July," Sam said.

"Yeah."

"Remember last year, when you swam around trying to get people to bring their boats to Mom's business so she wouldn't have to shut it down?"

Harbor laughed. "That was such a bad idea."

"We had a lot of bad ideas," Sam said.

"Especially when you and George stole a boat and nearly killed yourselves," Harbor added, and Sam started laughing, too, making Harbor laugh more.

Marina turned over in her sleep, and Sam and Harbor both held their breaths, trying to get as quiet as possible.

Marina didn't stir any more than that.

"George didn't come this summer. Sonny says he isn't going to come until Labor Day weekend, when their parents pick up Pork and Sonny," Sam said. "It's weird. Even if George was a jerk last year. It's weird that he used to swim in the lagoon with us all those summers and now he's not here at all."

"Yeah," Harbor said, swallowing around a sudden lump in her throat.

"Hey, Harbor?" Sam said. "Do you really want to go live with your dad?"

"You heard all that?" Harbor asked, even though she knew of course Sam had heard it. The entire house probably heard it, probably even the Badger brothers across the lagoon and Jamie Perez down the street. It was a small house on a small lagoon, and everyone could hear everything. That was the point of the fight in the first place, wasn't it? "I don't know. Maybe. Kind of. You and Marina would have more space if I did, you know."

"I know. But I never really thought about having that space. Because it's yours, so it's not like it's something missing," Sam said. "Does that make sense?"

"I don't know. But we should probably go to sleep."

"Oh. Yeah. Okay."

Harbor glanced over at Sam, who was staring up at the ceiling. "Do you . . . want me to stay?"

Sam didn't answer at first. But then she said, "Would you?"

"Just move over a little more."

Sam moved over a teeny tiny bit, then rolled over, and Harbor kept staring at the ceiling, too worried that if she rolled over, or moved at all, she would fall right out of the bed.

Harbor waited until she knew Sam was asleep before she closed her eyes and fell asleep, too.

CHAPTER TEN

On Sunrise Lagoon, the marshes spread out into the bay, which spread out into the ocean, which went on and on to the horizon. Boats drove by, and birds flew overhead, and Harbor could stand outside and see all of it. Every inch of Sunrise Lagoon.

Here, in the thick woods behind her dad's house, Harbor couldn't see past the giant trees. She was wearing a hat, her ponytail looped through the back to protect her hair from ticks, and as she looked up to find the sky above the trees, she felt small. It wasn't something she was used to feeling these days.

Quinn was standing beside her. She was the only reason Harbor was hiking to begin with. When she'd found out Harbor hadn't dared to explore the woods while chatting during practice that morning, Quinn had absolutely insisted.

When they started walking again, Harbor almost immediately tripped over a branch or a rock or a tree root. She stumbled, and Quinn reached out to steady her. "Careful." Quinn's voice was hushed, like always, but it was so quiet in the woods Harbor could hear her just fine.

"I don't think I'm a big fan of the woods." She definitely didn't have the right kind of shoes for this.

Quinn softly laughed. "I love the woods. We used to play in them all the time where I grew up in West Virginia. I like that the trees are always so much taller than me. I like that I'm not so *big* in the woods."

"I don't like feeling small," Harbor admitted.

"It's nice, sometimes," Quinn said. "Blending in, getting lost."

"You'd enjoy my house then," Harbor said, and then backtracked. "I mean, not here, with my dad. My other house, with my moms. My, uh, my mom and her . . . where I live with all my siblings. Anyway, I have four of them. It's easy to get lost in all the chaos."

"Oh wow," Quinn said. "Are you the oldest?"

"Yeah."

"I have an older brother. He's a lot older, though." Quinn sighed. "I don't see him much. He lives back home still. By *my* woods. I moved here to live with Aunt Dawn."

Harbor thought carefully about all the questions she wanted to ask. "Do you like living with your aunt?"

"I do, a *lot*," Quinn said. "Do you like living in both places?"

Harbor shrugged. "I don't really. I mostly live there. I'm here for the weekends. Just for now." She and Mom hadn't spoken about their fight. They hadn't really spoken much at all. All Harbor knew was that Mama said they were going to have a conversation with each other and with Harbor's dad, and they would talk to her about it again soon.

Soon hadn't happened yet.

"Sometimes I feel like things are too complicated," Harbor admitted. "My family at home. I have two moms. And two of my siblings are adopted. And my other mom, not the one who was with my dad, the other one, she gave birth to my youngest two siblings. And then there's me."

"You're the only one with a dad?" Quinn asked.

"Well, I mean, we all have dads, technically. I'm just the only one who knows mine," Harbor said, and then thought about her answer. "Though, it's a little more complicated with the twins? They used a sperm donor, so not really a dad. Biologically, I suppose?"

"I see what you mean," Quinn said. "My family . . ." She drifted off.

"You don't have to tell me," Harbor said, knowing it was probably difficult for Quinn to talk about, like it sometimes was for her. She didn't want to pry. "But you can, if you want to."

Quinn sighed. "My family is complicated, too. My dad, he's in prison. I never knew him. And then my mom isn't the best at taking care of me and my brother. My brother got a job as soon as he can, and he's been living on his own. Aunt Dawn took me in. She's adopted, by the way. Both her and my mom were."

It was maybe the most Quinn had said all at once to Harbor. "Thanks."

"For what?"

"For telling me? I have a hard time sometimes talking about my family. Just because I don't like explaining it always. And because sometimes people are . . . well."

"Yeah," Quinn said. "I get it."

"So, thanks. For telling me."

Quinn smiled. "Thanks to you, too. For telling me."

"Hey, Quinn?"

"Yeah?"

"Can we please go back to my dad's now?" Harbor asked. "I'd like to feel tall again."

Quinn laughed. "Yeah, okay. Come on, let's go."

Quinn took Harbor's hand and guided her out of the woods.

CHAPTER ELEVEN

Harbor was cranky come Sunday night. She had *long* basketball practices. Her legs were sore from trying to keep up with Quinn, and her voice was raspy from shouting she was open louder than Quinn would.

She felt a little guilty about that part. She wanted to prove to Coach Dawn she could start in their next game, but she felt bad using Quinn's weaknesses to do so. Quinn was her friend. Quinn was the first person outside Harbor's family who seemed to understand her.

It didn't help that Harbor hadn't slept well the night before. Harbor kept hearing the rustle of the trees blowing in the summer breeze, and she could see the shadows on the bedroom wall, and she kept thinking about getting smaller and smaller, the trees surrounding her and getting lost in them.

If there was ever a time for Marina's sound machine, last night was it. She'd even thought about finding a white noise app on her phone, but quickly decided that would be ridiculous. She *liked* not having to deal with all her siblings and all their noise and quirks at her dad's house.

Now Harbor was lying on her dad's couch, waiting for Mom to text her that she was there to pick her up. Her dad was in the kitchen, trying to get his dishwasher to work. It had stopped working when he tried to turn it on after dinner. Harbor suggested they just clean the plates—she didn't have a dishwasher at home, so she was used to it—but he was determined to fix it.

She glanced at her phone again to see if she'd missed Mom's text.

The doorbell rang.

Harbor didn't move to answer it. Her dad glanced out the kitchen window to see who it was. "Oh, it's Nadia," he said.

Mama. It was Mama.

Harbor's dad opened the door, and Mama stood there, smiling gently. "Hey, Doug."

"Chelsea get caught up in something?"

Mama nodded. "She was stuck at work, so I came."

"You got a car full of kids or something?"

"The neighbors are watching them," Mama clarified, and then she turned to look at Harbor. "Hey, you. Ready to go?"

"Harbor, go get your bag so Nadia doesn't need to wait on you."

Sometimes it felt like her dad purposely used Mama's name to avoid referring to her as one of Harbor's moms. If it was Mom at the door, he would have said "Harbor, go get your bag so your mom doesn't need to wait on you." At most, every so often, he would refer to Mama as Harbor's stepmom, but that sounded wrong.

Not wanting to leave the two of them alone, Harbor rushed to where she left her bag, grabbed it, and met Mama at the front door. "Okay. I'm ready."

"Can I get a hug?" her dad said, and Harbor leaned into him for a side hug. He then addressed Mama, "Tell Chelsea I'll call her tomorrow if she thinks we need to talk more or whatever."

"I still think you should come by for dinner so we can all talk in person," Mama said.

Harbor wanted to just leave now.

"If we need to talk in person, tell Chelsea we can do it the next time she picks Harbor up," Harbor's dad said, and then ended the conversation by turning back to Harbor. "I'll see you next weekend. Have a good week, kid."

"Bye, Dad."

Harbor and Mama got into the car and started driving in silence. Mama had the radio on low, though, which was something she did when she wanted to have a conversation and didn't want the music getting in the way. Harbor knew this, but she'd let Mama talk first.

Which, eventually, Mama did. "What I said, about your mom wanting to talk to your dad in person? It's nothing to worry about. We just want to talk more about what he said, and what you said. About living with him more full time."

Harbor shrugged.

"Your mom and I talked a lot about it this weekend, while you were here," Mama said. "Because, well, sometimes we need to talk things out before we can talk about them with you. Just about how we feel. What we think. I know you wish you could be part of those conversations, but as your moms, it's something we sometimes need to do just with the two of us first."

"Fine," Harbor said. "I get it."

"And *I* get it, Harbor. I get that you need privacy and space. I heard you, okay? We both did," Mama said, not taking her eyes off the road, even as Harbor turned to look at her. "I get that you're growing up. That basketball is more important to you than working on the boats these days. Your mom does, too."

Harbor sunk a little in her seat. "I still like the boats, I just . . ."

"I know," Mama said. "And your mom and I, we want to do what's best for you, whatever that is. And I hope you understand why you're too young to make this decision all on your own, and I hope you understand that there are reasons why the custody arrangement is what it is in the first place—"

"So the answer's still no," Harbor interrupted. "Just say that then."

"I'm not saying no," Mama said. "I'm saying . . . we're going to keep talking about it. We're going to think about it. And, considering everything, especially your attitude and the way you yelled at your mom, I think that's more than fair. Don't you?"

Harbor sighed. "Yeah. I guess. But I wish Mom would say this to me, too, instead of making you do it for her."

"Harbor . . ." Mama shook her head. "That's not what this is."

"Fine."

"We'll talk about it. All of us. Okay?" Mama said again. "But I need to ask. Is living with your dad really what you want? Or is being able to make that decision more important to you?"

"I just want to be left alone. Okay?" Harbor said. "That's all I want."

"Can you do me one favor, Harbor? Besides checking your attitude?" Mama asked.

Harbor rested her head against the car window. "What?"

"I need you to really think about what you want. Whatever that is, I can't promise you'll get it, but I *can* promise I'll do whatever I can, your mom and I both will, to make sure you're happy. So, think about it, hard. Okay?"

Harbor watched Mama carefully for a moment. She had a tight grip on the steering wheel. Her eyes were focused on the road in front of them, and Harbor wished they weren't driving so Mama could look at her instead.

Nadia.

Harbor wondered what it was like for her dad back then, when Mom fell in love with another woman. She wondered what it was like for Mama.

She wondered what would happen if she lived with her dad full time. Mom would always be Mom. But Mama . . . would things change between them if Harbor wasn't at Sunrise Lagoon? If she'd split time more evenly between her mom and dad growing up, if Dad had raised her a little more . . . would Mama have ever been more than *Nadia*?

It was too much to consider right now.

"Okay," Harbor said. "I'll think about it."

CHAPTER TWELVE

The Ali-O'Connors were playing Scrabble.

They always played in teams, except for Mama. She was too good at Scrabble to be on anyone's team, so they made her play by herself. She still won most of the time.

When Harbor and Mama arrived home, the rest of the Ali-O'Connors were sitting around the table with the Scrabble board in front of them. The teams appeared to be Mom and Cordelia (which meant Mom would be playing alone, because Cordelia did not have the attention span for Scrabble), Sam and Lir, and Marina playing solo. (Marina was second best, after Mama.)

They all looked up at the sound of the door. "Mama, hi, we're winning!" Cordelia said.

"*I'm* winning, you mean," Mom corrected.

"I told you to put down *fart*," Cordelia said.

Mom winked up at Mama and Harbor. "That is very true."

"What happened to my no crude language rule?" Mama said.

"*Fart* isn't crude."

"*Fart* totally is crude."

"Let's stop saying *fart*, please," Mama said.

"Mama, *please* come help us," Sam said.

"Lir and Sam are in last place."

"Lir keeps trying to put down huge words," Sam said.

"What's wrong with that?" Mama asked.

"I keep spelling them wrong," Lir lamented.

Mama gently squeezed Harbor's shoulder before crossing the room to put her bag down on the counter. She kissed the side of Mom's head, then crouched between Sam and Lir, seeing what letters they had to work with.

Mom glanced over at Harbor, offering her a small smile. "We just started. Come jump in."

"You can be on Marina's team," Cordelia said, moving the tiles around on her stand.

"*I* don't need anyone on my team, but if *you* need to be on my team, just know that I've already got my next two moves planned," Marina said.

"How do you have your next two moves planned if the rest of us haven't gone yet?"

"Just wait and watch me, Samantha."

"Come on," Mom said, again, holding out a hand. "Come play with us."

Harbor watched as Mama shuffled Lir and Sam's tiles until Sam's face lit up, and she started placing those tiles on the board.

Marina groaned. "Having Mama help is cheating!"

"They need the cheating, they're doing so bad," Cordelia pointed out.

Mom kept looking at Harbor.

Harbor didn't know what was stopping her from joining her family. "I think I'm gonna go shower and then hang in my room," she said.

Mom paused for a moment. "You sure?"

"Yeah," Harbor said. "I'm kind of tired."

Mom didn't look away, and Harbor didn't move yet, either.

But then Cordelia was tugging at Mom's shirt saying, "It's our turn, what about this word, is this how you spell it, can we put it over there by Marina's *T*?"

Mom, distracted, focused instead on the game.

Harbor shouldered her bag and headed down the hallway to her bedroom, leaving her family behind.

CHAPTER THIRTEEN

Mr. Martin was having a lagoon-wide barbecue. This wasn't unusual. He and Mr. Harris often went out on Mr. Martin's fishing boat, the *Lovely Lilah*, and came back with more fish or crabs or clams than the two of them could reasonably eat. Lir once asked why they didn't just stop fishing when they caught enough for the two of them. "We love an excuse for a party" was what Mr. Harris had replied.

The smell of buttery, flaky grilled fish wafted over to the Ali-O'Connors' backyard before they even made their way to Mr. Martin's. Everyone was in attendance. Everyone knew when Brenda Badger, with her husband and grandsons, arrived—her voice could be heard echoing throughout the entire lagoon. Boom was there by Marina's side, as always, but Boom's mom was not, also as always. Leisha Stewart, who lived a couple of lagoons over but always played poker with Mr. Martin and Mr. Harris (and, lately, Marina), was in charge of the grill. She kept pushing Mr. Martin out of the way, even though it was his fish and his grill. Mr. Martin let her take over.

The Perezes from across the lagoon were there, too, but their teenage daughter, Jamie, wasn't. First Jamie had stopped coming to these parties, and now George Badger was missing, too. Harbor wondered if turning into a proper teenager made you too cool for Sunrise Lagoon, for barbecues and family parties and longtime summer traditions.

Harbor was almost thirteen.

She leaned against the railing around Mr. Martin's deck and watched Mom on the dock, helping Cordelia and Lir set up the long floating rubber mat for the littlest kids to jump on and off. Once it was in the lagoon, Mom picked up Pork, the youngest of all the Sunrise Lagoon kids, and tossed him into the water while he squealed like a little pig. When Cordelia climbed back onto the dock, Mom quickly threw her right back in, too. Lir, learning from Cordelia's mistake, climbed onto the dock behind Mom and, without her noticing, pushed her right in.

She sputtered and splashed before turning around to point a finger at all three of the little ones. "Oh, you are *all* going down for that!"

"I remember when that was you." Mr. Martin came up behind Harbor, leaning beside her on the railing, watching

Mom and the kids. "Actually, I remember when your mama was one of the little fishes in the water."

"Mom," Harbor said.

"What?"

"Mama is the other one."

Mr. Martin laughed. "Regardless, I remember when she was the little one splashing and squealing in the water. And then there was you. And now them. I'm gonna miss it when you're all grown."

Mr. Martin had lived in Sunrise Lagoon, in the same house, longer than everybody, even Brenda Badger. He'd seen Mom grow up. Mom and Mr. Martin hadn't left, and as far as Harbor knew, neither one of them planned to.

Mr. Martin pointed over at Sonny and Sam, who were helping Leisha with the bucket of clams. "Maybe those two will continue the tradition for me, give me more little ones to watch swim in this lagoon for years to come."

Harbor made a face, ignoring the sinking feeling in her stomach because he'd paired Sonny with Sam instead of her. Even if she absolutely, *no way*, did not ever want babies with Sonny. "They're *twelve*, Mr. Martin."

He laughed. "You're right. I'm sorry. I shouldn't project."

Harbor had been avoiding Sonny. She was pretty sure Mama had noticed. She kept looking at the deck where Sonny and Sam, and Marina and Boom, were hanging out, and then looking back at Harbor.

Whatever. Harbor didn't want to think about Sonny. Or Sonny or Sam. Or little Badger-Ali-O'Connor babies.

She looked back out at the water, at Mom, who was floating on her back, her hair spread out behind her like blond seaweed, her eyes closed and the sun shining down on her. "What was she like?" Harbor asked. "My mom, I mean. When she was a kid."

"*Tough*," Mr. Martin said, and then laughed again. "A real rough and tumble tomboy. You did not tell that girl she couldn't do something. She would stick her nose up at you and jump headfirst into doing it, all with boat grease on her knees and cheeks. She used to give us all heart attacks on the daily, I swear that kid had a death wish. I think it was frustrating for her to be told no to all the things she loved. She used to scream at us from the docks as we drove away on the boats to go on long, grueling fishing trips."

"Why'd you all tell her no?" Harbor asked.

"Gender roles were a little different back then, kid. We learned a lot since. At least, I have. Your mom is the best boater I know, and sometimes I wonder how good she'd be if we let her start learning when she asked us, instead of having to do it all on her own."

Harbor thought about that. She considered her words very carefully, leaning even more into the railing to ask, as casually as she could, "What about my dad? What was she like with him?"

Harbor's dad didn't grow up in Sunrise Lagoon, but he lived close enough, in a house on one of the streets more inland. He went to the same school as Mom.

"He was her Sonny Badger, Harbor," Mr. Martin said. "He wasn't much of a boat kid, but he followed your mom anywhere. They were always together."

Harbor wondered when that changed.

She wondered what it meant for her friendship with Sonny.

Mama came up behind them, wrapping an arm around Harbor's shoulders. They were both sweaty from the sun, but neither seemed to mind it. "What're you two chatting about over here? Should I be nervous, Mr. Martin?"

"Just telling all the lagoon secrets to your daughter here," Mr. Martin "Gotta pass the torch to someone when I go."

"You are going nowhere," Mama promptly replied. "I believe the food is ready, if you two are hungry."

"I am starving," Mr. Martin said.

"Coming, Harbor?"

"Yeah," Harbor said.

She stayed where she was, though, a little longer, watching Mom swim in the lagoon until Mama called her and the kids out to get dinner.

After the moms said goodnight to all the kids, and Marina's sound machine had been turned on, and both Sam and Marina seemed to be sleeping, Harbor climbed back out of bed. She slowly made her way out of the room, closing the door gently behind her. Across the hall, under her moms' bedroom door, she could see the glow from the TV.

She knocked and waited.

"Come in," Mama called.

Harbor opened the door, slid in, closed the door behind her, and then leaned against it. Her moms were in bed, snuggled up and facing the TV. Harbor watched them carefully for a moment, the way Mom had an arm around Mama, and how Mama was resting a cheek on Mom's shoulder until Harbor had come in. Harbor couldn't explain it, but she really liked seeing the ways her moms, these two women, were in love with each other.

Mama muted the TV. "What's up, Harbor?"

She looked back and forth between them as they waited patiently for her to speak. "I was thinking about what you told me. I was thinking *like* you told me, I mean," Harbor said. "About . . . about what I wanted."

Mom turned to look at Mama, who nodded. "Okay. Where's your head at, Harbor?"

"My dad has no one to play Scrabble with," Harbor said.

"He . . . what?" Mom said, her forehead creasing.

"I mean, my dad, I think, wants to have me around more. To play Scrabble with, or whatever. I think it means a lot to him. And I like Coach Dawn. I like playing on the more competitive team." *Mostly*, Harbor thought, but her moms didn't need to know she was still bummed out about not starting in the games yet. "And, well. I know you said I don't get to choose, but you said to tell you what I wanted. And that's what I want. I want to stay at Dad's house."

Mom didn't move. Her expression didn't change.

Mama said, "Okay. Thank you for telling us. We, and your dad, have a lot to discuss still, to see what we feel is best. Okay?"

"Mom?" Harbor said, because Mom still hadn't moved.

Mom cleared her throat. "Yeah. I hear you, Harbor. I hear you, okay?"

Harbor wanted Mom to say more.

But she didn't.

"Okay."

CHAPTER FOURTEEN

This was what Harbor knew: When her mom and dad separated, her dad didn't take it too well. Mom and Harbor moved
back to Sunrise Lagoon, and her dad stayed in the house
they'd shared, until he didn't want to be there anymore. They
sold the house, and he moved in with his parents. Eventually,
he got an apartment, but he worked a lot because he didn't
want to be in the apartment alone, and he didn't have much
time for Harbor.

It made him too sad to see Mom or Harbor.

It all made Mom sad, too.

When he was finally ready to start spending time with
Harbor, they arranged the two weekends a month rule. They
hadn't adjusted it since, because it seemed to suit Harbor's
dad fine, and it seemed to suit Mom fine, and it honestly suited
Harbor fine, too. But her dad didn't work those long hours

anymore. And he wanted to spend more time with her now. And the plan that had worked for them before, maybe didn't work as well as it used to.

That was what Harbor's dad had said when Mom dropped Harbor off for the weekend. He said it all in one deep breath, like he'd rehearsed. "It doesn't suit us anymore, Chelsea. And I think the basketball team gives us a good excuse to make adjustments."

Mom didn't want to talk about it there, in front of Harbor, without Mama, but they started fighting a little bit anyway. At least here, at her dad's, Harbor had a room to escape to, where she could shut the door and be alone and drown out the sound of their voices.

Anyway, she had more important things to think about that weekend. They had another game, and Harbor was determined to play more than she had in the last one. She ran harder at practice, starting the minute she got to the gym, and was the last one off the court when Coach Dawn gave them a water break. For any of this to work—for her to get to play on a more competitive team, to keep playing with Quinn, to stay with her dad—Coach Dawn needed to think Harbor really was worthy of being on the team.

Once again, Harbor's family was not in the crowd at this game. There was no one to cheer loudly if she played well or played badly or just stood on the court doing nothing. It wasn't that they were too busy or something—Harbor hadn't told them. Maybe her dad had mentioned it, and maybe they could have asked since they knew she was playing basketball every weekend. But at the end of the day, they had not asked, and she had not mentioned it.

So they were not here.

Which was good. Which was fine.

She didn't start again anyway. She hadn't told them she wasn't starting. She didn't want them to drive all the way here when she barely even played, anyway. Harbor kept glancing at the scoreboard, at the clock as it counted down and down, and she still didn't go into the game.

She was in a foul mood when she finally did get subbed in. Quinn came out and smiled at her, sweaty and breathing heavy from the significant time she'd played. Harbor didn't smile back.

"Get out there, Harbor, bring this game home for us," Coach Dawn said, and Harbor didn't smile at her, either. She didn't respond to her at all.

And then Harbor wasted the minutes she did get to play by being absolutely terrible. She turned over the ball *twice*. She missed three shots and followed that by missing three foul shots, too. Camryn stopped passing her the ball, but it didn't matter, because Harbor couldn't hold her own on defense, either. She should have been able to get the rebound better than anyone—she was the currently tallest player on the court—but the other team kept pulling it from her grip.

Her dad was standing courtside, where he always stood, saying, "Come on, Harbor, you got this. Follow through!" But she didn't have this, she kept forgetting to follow through, and Coach Dawn yanked her out of the game and back onto the bench faster than she'd ever been pulled out of a game before.

Harbor was clenching her teeth hard when the game ended, and their team lost, and she hadn't gone back in at all. She sat with the rest of the team as Coach Dawn sternly explained everything they could have done better. "Harbor, you have to practice those free throws," she said.

"If I played more, I'd have made more," Harbor snapped back.

She couldn't help herself.

Even if she knew better.

Even if the quiet gasps from her teammates and the way Fiona whispered "*Ooooh*" meant the rest of the team knew better, too.

"What did we talk about? You have a role on this team, Harbor. So watch your tone, and start thinking about that. Think about your place on this team," Coach Dawn said. "Not everyone in college or the WNBA starts. Not everybody plays significant minutes. But they know their role and what their job is and how to support their team. You played badly because you weren't thinking about the team."

Now Harbor was clenching her jaw hard to keep from crying, *and* she was embarrassed, too.

Coach Dawn dismissed them, and Harbor waited for everyone else to leave first, not wanting to walk with her team, not wanting to face them.

Quinn lagged behind. "It's okay to have a bad game," she said softly.

"I know," Harbor gritted out through her teeth.

"You'll have a good game next time."

"Quinn? Can we just . . . not talk?" Harbor said, trying and failing not to snap at her, too. "I just . . . need a minute. To sit here and not talk. Can that be okay?"

"Yes," Quinn said quickly. She didn't say anything else. Instead, she sat down next to Harbor. She waited quietly and patiently, reaching out to hold Harbor's hand.

It felt nice. It also made Harbor want to cry even more, though she wasn't entirely sure why.

Still, Harbor intertwined her fingers with Quinn's as she sat there breathing into the silence.

Harbor didn't talk much that evening with her dad, either. She kept thinking about sitting there, with Quinn's hand in hers, and how much she loved how sturdy and calm and quiet Quinn was. How much Quinn seemed to understand without Harbor having to say anything.

Her friendship with Sonny was like that. Or it used to be at least.

Every single summer for as long as she remembered, Harbor would get really excited to see Sonny when he finally arrived. She would count down the days until Memorial Day weekend, when Sonny and his brothers would drive down to their grandparents' house where they would spend the entire summer. She would hear Sonny's parents' car pull into the driveway across the lagoon, and she would run, or swim, or get over there as fast as possible because she missed him.

It was the same with Quinn now. Harbor found she was excited for the weekends, she looked forward to going to practice—she would be ready at least fifteen minutes earlier than they needed to be—because Quinn was her friend and she missed her during the week. It wasn't exactly the same as spending an entire school year apart from one another, but a week was still long, and Harbor still got butterflies knowing that when Friday came, she'd see Quinn the next day.

It was the same thing. It was the same as with Sonny.

Though, maybe it was a little different, too. Harbor had never held Sonny's hand and thought about how smooth it felt, thought about how nice it fit in hers. She never thought about how much she liked Sonny's laugh and how much *she* wanted to be the one to make him smile.

Sure, Sonny was her best friend and she liked being the one he wanted to spend the most time with—even if that had changed because of Sam—but Harbor didn't catch herself watching Sonny like she watched Quinn.

Maybe it wasn't actually the same at all.

"You feeling okay? You're quiet," Harbor's dad said.

"I'm fine," Harbor said, even if her thoughts were making her kind of sweaty. "Just tired."

"Do you know who's picking you up tonight? Your mom or Nadia?"

"My mom," Harbor said, and then cringed a little. *They're both my moms.*

Her dad focused back on the cold leftover pizza they were eating. Harbor had never eaten pizza cold, but she found out that she was a very big fan of it.

But even still, she just picked at the cheese. She couldn't stop thinking about Sonny and Sam. She couldn't stop thinking about Quinn. "Hey, Dad? When did you first get a girlfriend?" Harbor found herself asking.

Her dad groaned a little. "I think I asked your mom to dance with me at the eighth-grade dance. Does that count?"

"Oh. Okay."

"Oh god, you'll be in eighth grade soon, won't you," her dad said, shuddering. "Guess I should start preparing myself for boys to be asking you to dance, too, huh?"

Harbor shrugged. She swallowed the bite of pizza she was chewing on. "I guess. Or maybe not. Maybe, I mean." She paused again. "Maybe I'm not so interested in boys."

Her dad laughed. It didn't really sound right. "Focus on your school and focus on basketball for now. That's all you need to worry about." He tossed his napkin into his empty plate. "All right, I'm stuffed. I'm gonna start cleaning up this mess."

He stood up, gathering the empty pizza box and their dirty paper plates before heading into the kitchen.

Harbor didn't bring up boys or girls for the rest of the night. She didn't think she'd ever bring it up again.

CHAPTER FIFTEEN

Harbor sat on the floor in the living room, trying to keep Good Boy's slobber away from her new sneakers while she laced them up, ignoring the way Mom kept huffing. When Harbor showed the shoes her dad had bought to Mom, her first reaction was "Wow, those are awesome," followed almost immediately by "But what was wrong with your old sneakers?"

There was nothing wrong with her old sneakers, really. They were a Christmas present—not this last Christmas, the one before it. They were getting a little worn, but not terribly so. She'd asked for them, and she'd surprised when she opened the box on Christmas morning. She thought they were too expensive—they were more expensive than the brands her moms usually bought her—but there they were, sitting underneath the Christmas tree.

The ones her dad just bought her were even better, and brand new, and she was excited to lace them up and break them in so they would be ready for the weekend. Maybe they would give her the little extra *oomph* she needed.

Or maybe they would just add to the ever-growing list of things to fight about between her parents.

Harbor, as she finished lacing her sneakers, could *feel* Cordelia staring at her before she looked up and saw her. Cordelia was leaning against the couch, not saying anything, just *looking*.

"What?" Harbor snapped as Good Boy stuck his snout into one of the sneakers, and Harbor tried again to move him away. "Get off, Good Boy."

"Nothing!" Cordelia said, then added much more quietly, in a way that reminded Harbor of Quinn, "Sorry."

"Sorry for what?"

"I'm just sorry!"

Cordelia took off out of the room, and Harbor rolled her eyes, deciding to ignore it. Cordelia always had been the weirdest of all the Ali-O'Connor siblings; there was no point in trying to understand her.

Good Boy bit the laces of Harbor's sneakers and tugged. "Good Boy! I said get *off*!"

He didn't immediately let go of the sneaker, and Harbor tugged it from his mouth with one hand, using the other hand to push him away. He cried, dropping the sneaker, and hopping away from her, tail between his legs. He looked at her with his puppy dog eyes, scurried to the other side of the room, and curled onto his dog bed.

Mama, who was in the kitchen, saw the whole thing. "Harbor!"

"He wouldn't stop! He's been all over me all day!"

"He's a dog and he loves you," Mama said. "You've been gone all weekend and he's excited you're home. There are better ways to handle him trying to get at your things."

"Whatever."

"Not *whatever*! You're not a little kid anymore, Harbor, stop acting like one."

"Whoa, what's going on in here?" Mom asked, coming into the room. Good Boy lifted his head and whined when he saw her. She sat on the ground next to his dog bed and let him slobber all over her.

"Great, you're taking the dog's side over mine, too," Harbor said.

"Dogs don't get cranky and snarky as they get older." Mom stuck her tongue out at Harbor. "They are much more pleasant on the regular than my children are."

Harbor glared at her. "Real nice, Mom."

"Lir! Stop! Leave me alone!" Marina yelled from the other room.

"Oh, come on, what now," Mom groaned.

Harbor thought it was actually really nice to hear someone else getting annoyed.

"You know what?" Mama said, throwing the dishrag onto the kitchen counter. Her face was set with determination. "We all need to get out of this house and do something. As a family."

Mom perked up immediately. "Yeah! Okay. Boat ride?"

"Beach?" Mama countered.

"Yes! Okay! I'll get everything ready," Mom said, popping up from the floor. Good Boy's ears perked up, too. "You gather the troops!" Mom basically ran out of the room, which had Harbor rolling her eyes all over again. The summer sometimes turned Mom into a child.

Mama made her way over to Harbor, gently tugging her ponytail. "I feel like we haven't gotten to do any of the big summer things as a family with you yet this year," she said. "So, what do you say? A beach day? For me?"

Well, it wasn't like Harbor was going to say no to that.

Especially since she wasn't sure what would happen to family days with Mama if she *did* get to live with her dad full time.

"Fine. Yeah, okay."

The problem was that a *family* beach day always turned into: "Can we invite Pork!" and "I want to bring Boom!" and

"What about Sonny?" And then there were ten of them carefully getting onto Mom's boat. Mom made sure they all had life jackets, and Mama made sure they all took their seats, and Mom got a little stressed as she also loaded the beach chairs and towels and umbrella Mama begged her to bring.

It always made Mom a little on edge to have a full boatload of Ali-O'Connors and their friends.

Which put Harbor on edge a little, because maybe they should have just taken a family trip like Mama had suggested to begin with. No Boom, squishing her into the hard side of the boat. No Sonny, avoiding her gaze as he sat with his little brother in the back of the boat with Cordelia.

At least they'd left Good Boy at home.

"Cordelia, sit down!" Marina screeched as they made their way quickly across the bay.

"Sorry!" Cordelia quickly responded.

"I don't know about this," Marina said, for the hundredth time. "There's too many of us. You can't keep eyes on all of us."

Then why did you invite Boom? Harbor thought, but kept her mouth shut.

"Mama and I are both here and can watch all of you. And we all know the rules, yes?" Mom said, taking her eyes off the bay for a moment to glance next to her, where Cordelia was sitting. "Yes, Cordelia?"

Cordelia sunk a little in her seat. "No wandering."

"No wandering."

"I haven't wandered since last year," she weakly defended herself.

It was a habit they were all relieved Cordelia seemed to be growing out of—finally. They'd previously lost track of her at the grocery store, at school, at the dentist, and one very memorable time last summer at the very beach they were currently headed to.

"And for that we are grateful," Mom said. "Let's keep up the good work."

Everyone, on Mom's orders, got really quiet as she pulled the boat into Tices Shoal. It wasn't as crowded today, a weekday, as it was on the weekends or the Fourth of July. Still, there were a lot of boats docked in the water, and a lot of people swimming, and Mom wanted to be safe and focused as she navigated them close to the ladder that led to the beach.

Once the boat was docked, Mom got off first. The bay water came up to her thighs. Mama passed her the floating cooler, which Mom dropped into the water and put the beach bag and chairs on top of it. Harbor, Sam, and Sonny all got off next. The water came up high on Sam's and Sonny's thighs and just barely covered Harbor's knees. Harbor took the umbrella, and Sonny and Sam helped Boom and Marina into the water. Mama, the twins, and Pork went last. The little ones, all in their life vests, had to swim.

It was a train of Ali-O'Connors and Badger brothers and Boom making their way the short distance from the boat to the ladder that led to the beach.

They were able to find a spot nice and close to the ocean, but far enough away that when the tide came in the water wouldn't drench all their things. They also were nice and close to the lifeguard stands so that anyone who wanted to swim would have extra eyes on them in the ocean.

Sonny helped Mom get the umbrella situated into the sand nice and deep, making sure it wouldn't blow over in the wind, while Mama set up the beach chairs. Marina and Harbor each splayed out a towel to lay on.

Mom found a big shell in the sand and put it on top of Pork's head like a hat. Pork immediately kicked around the sand looking for a shell to retaliate. Lir was helping him, until Mom started tickling Lir. "Race you to the water?" Mom said.

"Oh heck yeah, me too!" Boom said.

"Careful, please!" Mama called from her spot in one of the beach chairs as Lir, Pork, Boom, Sonny, and Sam all took off toward the ocean. Marina followed more slowly, staying closer to shore and letting the waves lap at her feet while the others all dove in. Cordelia sat in the other beach chair and leaned over to bury her feet and legs in the sand.

"You're not going in?" Mama asked, turning to look at Cordelia.

"Not right now," Cordelia said.

Harbor, who hadn't said one word to Sonny since the boat and had no plans to join him in the water, lay back on her beach towel, closed her eyes and let the heat from the sun kiss her face.

Mama gently kicked Harbor's leg with her bare foot. "You want to tell me what's going on between you and Sonny?" she asked.

Harbor sighed. She knew Mama had noticed. "Nothing. I just don't feel like hanging out with him all the time."

"Did something happen?"

"No."

"Are you lying to me?"

"Mama, stop."

"All right, all right. I'll let it go," Mama said, settling in her chair and letting her head fall back to enjoy the sun on her face, too. "But I hope you know you can talk to me about anything."

Harbor rolled over to tan her back.

This proved to be a mistake when, moments later, she felt something—a bunch of small somethings—being placed on her back. She picked her head up to see Cordelia kneeling next to her in the sand, reaching over to place another small something on top of Harbor. "What are you doing?" Harbor asked.

"Making you a mermaid," Cordelia said quietly.

It was strange, not because Cordelia was putting things on her—she always did this sort of thing, like make sandcastles on Mama's toes or bury Lir shoulders deep in the sand—but because Cordelia never did anything quietly.

Harbor felt a little too hot under the summer sun. "Why are you being so weird?"

"I am not," Cordelia said.

She was, though, and Harbor groaned. She didn't want to deal with it. She got up on her hands and knees, the little shells that Cordelia had placed on her back hanging on until Harbor stood up and they all cascaded down onto the towel. She shook a little, not unlike Good Boy after he got wet, bits of sands flying off her.

"Okay, well, this mermaid now needs to rinse off," she said, and then quickly reached to grab Cordelia around the waist. "And she's taking you to the depts of the ocean floor with her."

Cordelia immediately started giggling and squirming. It made carrying her difficult. Cordelia wasn't little anymore. She had long limbs, longer than Lir's, and Harbor was hoping Cordelia would end up tall like her, too. She half-carried, half-dragged Cordelia to the water, catching Mama's eyes, who smiled at them.

As they passed where Marina was standing, Harbor said, "Help me toss this little sea witch into the water."

"No, no, no!" Cordelia yelled, but she was smiling and she'd stopped trying to get away, clearly excited to be thrown into the ocean.

Marina reached for Cordelia's feet and walked farther into the water with Harbor so they could start swinging her. "One," Harbor counted.

"Two," Marina said.

"Mom! Lir! Avenge me!" Cordelia shouted.

Harbor and Marina flung Cordelia into the ocean. She splashed around and immediately swam over to where Pork, Lir, and Mom were ducking under the waves. Boom body-surfed practically into Harbor, who jumped out of the way at the last second. Boom flopped around the wet sand like a beached whale for a second before getting up and standing next to Marina.

"Let's go lay out for a bit," Marina said. Boom agreed, and the two of them went back to the towel that Harbor had just abandoned.

Sonny and Sam bodysurfed over right after.

"You coming in?" Sonny tugged at the bottom of his swim shorts that were clinging to his legs.

"Maybe," Harbor said. She thought about jumping in quickly so she didn't have to stand here with Sonny and Sam.

"Are you still mad at me?" Sonny asked.

Sam looked between the two of them. "Why, were you two fighting?"

"It's none of your business, Sam," Harbor snapped.

"Sorry."

"You don't need to be mean about it," Sonny said.

Of course Sonny would take Sam's side. He used to take Harbor's side over anyone else's. *That* was what best friends did. "You don't need to constantly do and say everything for Sam."

Sonny blushed, immediately, his face turning bright pink.

"Is everything okay?" Sam asked, twisting her fingers nervously in front of her.

"Everything is fine?" Sonny said. "I mean, it is! Everything is fine. We should just go swimming? Okay?" He reached out for Sam's hand.

Sam let him hold it.

Did Sam like the way Sonny's hand felt in hers as much as Harbor's liked Quinn's?

And what did it mean if she did?

Harbor's stomach started hurting.

"So what? Are you boyfriend and girlfriend now?" Harbor asked.

Sonny immediately let go of Sam's hand.

Sam's forehead got all wrinkly. "What?"

"Sonny *likes* you, Sam."

The crashing of the waves seemed impossibly loud in Harbor's ears, and Sonny and Sam got exceptionally quiet. Sam blinked. "Oh," she said.

Sonny was still bright pink, only now his face was all scrunched up, too. "Why would you say that!" he yelled, louder than Harbor had ever heard him yell before.

Harbor didn't know why she would say that.

She *shouldn't* have said that. She knew she shouldn't have.

"You're a terrible friend, Harbor!" Sonny said, his eyes watery. "And you know what? You're a terrible sister, too."

He shoved past her, bumping into her shoulder as he stormed over to where Marina, Boom, and Mama were sitting in the sunshine.

Harbor didn't follow him.

Neither did Sam. She eyed Harbor carefully. "I didn't know."

Harbor didn't want to talk about it anymore. She stormed away from Sam, back toward their spot on the beach. She lay on her back on her towel, on the opposite side of where Sonny was sitting in the sand. She didn't move for the next three hours.

She was sunburned by the time they left.

CHAPTER SIXTEEN

"What's got your goat today?"

Camryn walked over and stood next to Harbor, looking at her carefully while she asked the question. Harbor had just missed her fifth foul shot in a row. The team was taking turns practicing shooting free throws. Anyone who hit ten in a row got to stop and take a water break. Camryn was almost there. So was Quinn.

"What's *got my goat*?" Harbor asked.

Camryn cringed. "I was trying to be funny."

"She's not very good at it," Fiona chimed in. She shot the ball, making her seventh in a row.

"You're close!" Camryn said.

"Don't jinx me!"

Harbor let herself fade into the background as Camryn and Fiona debated the logistics of what counted as a jinx, and if talent mattered more, and which one of them would make it to ten first.

They would both make it to ten before Harbor, at least. Probably the entire team would. The other girls all seemed so much better than she was. They went to Olympic camps or had dads who were professional coaches or had sisters who were recruited to play for UConn. Geena wore a UConn sweatshirt the other day, even though it was ninety degrees out, because she was so happy for her sister *and* told everyone she would absolutely play basketball at UConn, too.

Some of the best basketball players went to UConn.

Diana Taurasi went to UConn.

Meanwhile, Harbor was still trying to convince her moms to let her play for Dawn's AAU during the school year.

No wonder she wasn't starting.

"Hey, are you okay?" Quinn's voice was suddenly interrupting her thoughts. It made Harbor jump. She blushed when Quinn laughed. "I don't think I've ever startled anyone before, but I'm not surprised. You're in your head. You aren't shooting so great today. What's wrong?"

"I never shoot good free throws." Harbor scowled.

"During games you sometimes miss," Quinn agreed, which made Harbor blush even more. "But in practice you usually do better."

"How do you know that?"

"I just pay attention, I guess."

Harbor couldn't blush more if she tried. "Just got a lot on my mind. I guess it's affecting my game? Maybe? I don't know."

"Harbor? Quinn? How're those shots going?" Coach Dawn called over, which was her nice way of telling them to stop talking and start shooting.

Harbor passed the ball to Quinn, who lined up to take a shot. Harbor watched her carefully. She watched where Quinn placed her feet—her left foot a little ahead of her right foot, perfectly placed in front of the foul line—and how she bent her knees, bouncing a little bit. She watched as Quinn quickly slicked one of the strands of hair that fell out of her ponytail behind her ear before lining the ball up with her hands. She bent her knees even more and took the shot.

It went through the basket with a beautiful *swish*.

"Was that ten? I think you're done," Harbor said.

"I think only eight. I'll keep shooting."

Harbor was pretty sure Quinn was just being nice. It was definitely ten.

"Hey, so. My aunt got me tickets to see a New York Liberty game," Quinn said, and Harbor's chest immediately squeezed with intense jealousy. The New York Liberty was Harbor's favorite WNBA team. She went to the foul line to take her shot.

"That's *awesome*," Harbor said, and she meant it.

"Would you— Do you maybe want to come?"

Harbor was so startled she shot the ball quickly and wildly and thought for sure it would air ball. Instead, it miraculously swished right through the net.

"Nice shot," Quinn said.

"Are you serious?"

"Yeah, it arched beautifully and went right through the net?"

"No, I mean about the basketball game!"

"Oh," Quinn said, stepping up to the foul line to take her turn as Harbor retrieved the ball and passed it over to her. "Yes. Do you want to?"

"I would love to!"

Coach Dawn blew the whistle. "All right. Get some water, nice shooting, everyone."

Harbor trailed after Quinn as they made their way to the bench. "When's the game? I have to ask my dad. I'll do that as soon as he picks me up. How much was the ticket? Do you know where the seats are? Have you ever been to a game before?"

"Um. That was a lot of questions. You don't need to pay me, my aunt bought me the tickets and said I could bring whoever I wanted. I think they're okay seats? My aunt takes me to games sometimes, so yeah, I've been." Quinn counted off her fingers trying to make sure she answered them all. "Oh, and the game is two Wednesdays from now. Not next week, the week after."

Wednesday. That wasn't a Dad day.

"Oh," Harbor said.

"You can't go?" Quinn said, her shoulders slumping as she picked up on Harbor's disappointment.

Harbor shook her head. "I don't know, but don't give the ticket to anyone else. I'll figure it out."

It wasn't often that Harbor managed to *think* before speaking her mind, but she wanted to go to the New York Liberty game with Quinn more than anything, so she knew she had to be strategic about it.

She knew Mom would appreciate if she came to her before her dad—especially since Mom was still a little mad at Harbor's dad for speaking with Harbor first about living with him—so she thought really hard about what she wanted to say and approached Mom after dinner. Mom usually was happiest after a meal.

"Mom, I'd like to ask you something."

Mom's eyebrows rose up high on her forehead. "And so formally, too. Do you want to walk Good Boy with me and ask?"

Good Boy was in his bed in the corner. He lifted his head up at his name, then looked over at Harbor and whined. Goody Boy still seemed wary of Harbor. When she'd arrived home after the weekend away, instead of barreling toward her like the big lug he was, Good Boy avoided her. She'd been grateful in the moment because she was carrying her basketball bag, but he hadn't approached her since, either.

She'd try to remember to rub his belly later.

She focused back on Mom. "No, let me just ask you right now, like I said."

"How quickly your politeness turned to attitude."

Harbor sighed, then took a deep breath and tried again. "Okay. Sorry. I'm just worried. Because Quinn, my friend on my basketball team, she asked me to go to a New York Liberty game with her. And oh my god, Mom, I really want to go. You know I really want to go. You wouldn't even need to pay for the ticket! It would be paid for! By her aunt! Who is my basketball coach! So please can I go?"

Mom narrowed her eyes. "What's the catch? Why are you so worried to ask me?"

"Oh." Harbor almost forgot the important part. "It's Wednesday. Next week. And so, I was thinking maybe I could just spend the whole week at Dad's? Instead of you picking me up on Sunday night, and then driving me to Quinn's to go to the game on Wednesday, and then picking me up, and then taking me back again on Friday?"

Mom didn't respond right away.

"I haven't asked Dad yet," Harbor quickly added. "I wanted to talk to you first."

Mom nodded slowly. "I really appreciate that," she said, just like Harbor hoped she would.

And then, after a moment of silence went by that almost killed Harbor with anticipation, Mom said, "Okay."

"Okay?" Harbor asked, a little stunned.

"I mean, I think it sounds fine. I'd have to run it by your dad, to make sure he's okay with it, but I think that's fair," Mom said.

"Really?"

Mom softly laughed. "Yeah, Harbor. Really."

Harbor quickly rushed over to Mom, wrapping her arms around her in the closest thing to a bear hug Harbor would dare give anyone. Mom's laugh turned surprised, and she immediately hugged Harbor back, holding onto her tightly and burying her face in Harbor's hair. When Harbor moved to pull away, Mom didn't let go. "One more second," Mom said, holding tight. "Just give me one more second."

Harbor let her have that second. Considering how excited Harbor was about the basketball game, she'd have let Mom have thirty entire minutes if she asked for it.

When Mom finally let her go, Harbor wasted no time. Her phone was charging next to her bed, and she wanted to let Quinn know that, while Mom still had to talk to her dad, Harbor was pretty sure she'd be able to come with her to the game.

She made it to the hallway right outside her bedroom when she ran into Cordelia. Cordelia stood at the threshold of Harbor's bedroom, standing in the way. "Cordelia, move."

Cordelia did not move.

Harbor pushed around her. Luckily, Marina was at Boom's, and Harbor didn't know where Sam was. Probably with Sonny. Harbor didn't care.

Cordelia stayed in the doorway. "I don't want you to go."

"What?" Harbor said, preoccupied with reaching for her cell phone and yanking it off the charger.

"Please don't go."

Harbor glanced up when she heard the quiver in Cordelia's voice. "Go where?" Harbor asked, confused. "The basketball game?"

"I don't want you to live with your dad," Cordelia said.

Harbor sighed. "Cordelia . . ."

"I'll be better, I promise," Cordelia said. "I'll grow up. I won't do any more experiments. I won't touch your things. I *promise* I'll grow up."

"Cordelia," Harbor tried to interrupt.

"I don't want you to go!" Cordelia said again.

And then she started crying. Heaving sobs as she stood in the doorway wiping furiously at her eyes, like she was angry at herself for the tears falling down her face. She cried and pressed her hands to her eyes, her breath coming in big heaves as she tried to make herself stop.

Harbor stared, wide-eyed at Cordelia, not knowing what to do.

"What's going on?" Mom came from down the hall.

"What's wrong? What happened?" Mama said, coming right behind her.

Cordelia couldn't catch her breath to answer either of them. Lir suddenly appeared out of nowhere, shoving between their moms, and Harbor could hear the back door open and close, which meant more of her siblings were home now, too.

"She doesn't want me to go to my dad's," Harbor said. She couldn't take her eyes off Cordelia.

"I'm stopping! I'm not crying!" she said while crying.

Mama knelt down next to her, rubbing her back. "Let's go talk in your room for a bit, okay? How's that sound?"

Cordelia let Mama lead her out of the doorway and into her own room. Lir shifted from foot to foot, not knowing whether to follow Cordelia or not. Sam and Marina appeared in the doorway, too, everyone wanting to know what was happening. Mom hugged Lir. "Cordelia's just a little confused," Mom said. "Harbor's been spending a lot of time at her dad's, but that doesn't mean she's not going to be around here, okay? We're a family. Family sticks together, wherever we are, right?"

Everyone slowly nodded their heads.

"Is Harbor gonna live with her dad all the time instead?" Lir asked.

"She is?" Marina asked. "When?"

"You don't need to worry about any of that, okay?" Mom said. "Harbor's gonna spend next week at her dad's, but she'll be back after that."

It was the truth. But Harbor knew Mom was leaving out a lot of details.

"Would she take her Diana Taurasi poster with her?"

"Marina, hush," Sam said.

"Look, why doesn't everyone go wash up for dinner? Mama's making stuffed eggplant, I know that's a favorite of yours, Lir," Mom said. "Sam, can you set the table, please?"

Harbor's siblings all quietly did as they were told, leaving Harbor and Mom alone.

"I didn't . . . I didn't say anything to her. About wanting to live with my dad. I don't know why she got all upset," Harbor said.

Mom shrugged. "You've said it yourself over and over again. The house is small. They hear you, Harbor."

"I didn't mean for her to get upset."

Mom smiled sadly, reaching forward to push a loose strand of hair out of Harbor's face. "I know," she said. "Why don't you get ready for dinner, too, okay?"

"Yeah. Okay."

Mom turned and walked away, leaving Harbor alone.

CHAPTER SEVENTEEN

Harbor couldn't remember the last time she spent a weekday with her dad. The arrangement had always been weekends. Until, well, now.

Which was why waking up at her dad's house on Monday morning was so different. For starters, her dad didn't work on the weekends. While he mostly worked from home—he had an IT job at a local university—he had to go in that day for a team meeting. Harbor, of course, was old enough to be left home alone for a few hours, but it was very rare that she was ever *actually* home alone.

There was always a sibling or two or three or four, or a giant dog, left behind with her.

Her dad left before she woke up, and Harbor enjoyed leisurely getting out of bed without someone waking her up for basketball practice, or because they wanted to go swimming in the bay, or because Good Boy needed to go out and Mom walked so hard everyone heard her every step, or because Cordelia was awake and the entire lagoon needed to know it. (*Don't think about Cordelia*, she told herself. Thinking about Cordelia here, at her dad's house, made Harbor's stomach hurt.)

She stretched went into the kitchen, where she poured herself a bowl of cereal without having to help anyone else pour theirs, too. She took a seat at the table alone, where she was able to eat in silence.

She left the bowl in the sink to clean later, because there was no one to tell her not to. She made her way to the bathroom, where she didn't have to wait for anyone else who might be using it and took the longest shower of her life. She could do that, too, because no one was waiting, and no one would bang on the door to tell her she was using all the hot water.

Even though she was definitely using all the hot water.

And then she settled on the couch in front of the TV, where she could choose whatever she wanted to watch and watch it for however long she wanted to.

She lasted an hour and a half before she got bored.

Her dad wouldn't be home for another two hours.

Harbor turned off the TV and went to look out the window. None of the neighbors were outside. Which was good, because Harbor didn't know any of these neighbors. Not like at Sunrise Lagoon, where she knew everyone. Usually, one of the neighbors would know that Harbor was home alone—her moms would tell someone to keep an eye on her. Here, no one knew anything.

On the other side of the house was the backyard and the thick woods, and Harbor didn't want to look at those woods for very long. Quinn might like the woods, but Harbor, when she glanced at them, saw way too many moving shadows.

She considered calling Mom, just to check in, but she decided not to. She didn't want Mom to think she couldn't handle being here during the week. She had to prove that the week would be fine and good and perfect.

She could handle two more hours alone.

When Harbor's dad *did* come home, it wasn't exactly a relief. He was cranky. He was tired from his team meeting. "I can't watch a movie right now, Harbor, I have work to do," he said. "And I need you to please turn the TV down."

"I won't be able to hear it."

"Fine, I'm going to go work at the desk in the guest room."

"But all my stuff is in there."

"Harbor, I can't argue with you right now over every little thing!"

Harbor felt her face flush. "Don't talk to me like that! I didn't do anything!"

"Don't talk to *me* like that!" he snapped back at her. "I'm your father, Harbor. And I need to get things done, so just go quietly watch TV and let me work!"

Harbor clenched her jaw as he took his laptop and shut the door to the guest bedroom—her bedroom—a little harder than necessary, leaving her alone again. She didn't like getting yelled at by her dad. He so rarely ever yelled. That was Mom's job, or Mama's. They were the ones to scold Harbor if she didn't do her homework, or got into a fight with one of her siblings, or ran on the back deck. When she was with her dad, on the weekends, there was no reason for her to get in trouble. Not when all she did was play basketball and hang out with him.

When her dad finished working, they didn't "talk it out" like Mama would have made her. Mama would have come out of the bedroom, explained why she got mad, and made Harbor tell her all the reasons she got mad, too.

Her dad made hot dogs and beans (Harbor hated beans) and they didn't talk about their fight at all. It was like her dad had forgotten it happened.

He didn't need to go into the office on Tuesday, but he did need to work and he shut himself in the guestroom again. It made Harbor feel both in the way and displaced without a place of her own. Plus, there was nothing on TV except morning talk shows, news, and soap operas.

She decided to bite the bullet and call Mom. She said to "check in," after all.

That was all Harbor was doing. Checking in.

Someone she *thought* was Mom answered on the third ring, which was two rings too many for Harbor. Almost immediately she realized it was Mama's voice, even though Harbor had called Mom's cell phone. "Hey, you," Mama said. "Is everything okay?"

"Everything's okay. Where's Mom?"

"She and Mr. Martin took everyone fishing," Mama said.

"Oh," Harbor said. "Even Marina?"

"Believe it or not, even Marina." Mama laughed. "Boom's enthusiasm has ended up being a good influence, I have to admit."

Harbor didn't care about Boom. "Even Lir went?" Lir hated fish guts.

"Yep," Mama said. "It's just Good Boy and me here."

Like it was just Harbor here, right now, even though her dad was in the other room. "Oh."

"I'll tell them you called. Your mom might want to call to check in later."

"That's why I called," Harbor said. "To check in. Everything is good, though. If she doesn't want to call. You can tell her I'm fine."

"I will." Harbor could hear Mama's smile in her voice. "When's the basketball game?"

"Tomorrow night," Harbor said.

"Will you call and tell me all about it?" Mama asked.

Harbor swallowed around a sudden lump in her throat. "Can I?"

The guest room door suddenly creaked open, and Harbor turned quickly to see her dad finally emerge from it. She paused, feeling kind of like she'd been caught stealing cookies after bedtime, but she didn't know why.

"Please do," Mama answered her.

"Who's on the phone?" her dad asked. "Your mom?"

"Yeah," Harbor lied. Only, it wasn't a lie. Only, in her dad's mind it was. In any case, Harbor knew he thought she meant Mom, and she didn't correct him. To Mama she said, "I gotta go. I'll talk to you later."

"I'll talk to you later, sweetheart," Mama said. "I love you."

Harbor had asked Mom if she could spend the week at her dad's. Mom had talked to dad about it, and they had decided she could. They didn't ask Mama. Harbor hadn't thought to ask Mama, either.

The lump in Harbor's throat felt bigger. "Love you, too."

When she hung up, her dad was still looking at her. "What'd your mom want?" he said. He was smiling, but Harbor felt like she'd done something wrong. "Checking in on us?"

"Just checking in," Harbor said.

"Want to go get something to eat? There's nothing here for lunch."

Harbor nodded. "Yeah, okay."

Her dad grabbed his keys, and Harbor tried not to think about Mama or Cordelia or anyone else the rest of the day.

Wednesday finally came. Harbor was starting to think maybe it never would. The thought of spending two more weekdays *and* a weekend with her dad kept making her stomach hurt, and she didn't know what that meant. She was happy here. She had space here. This week, this whole week, was exactly what Harbor had told her moms she wanted.

Maybe she was just having an off week. That happened sometimes. Harbor was moody—everyone knew that. Even Harbor knew that. Sometimes she just didn't want to deal with people, and sometimes she was just cranky, and that was just who she was. So maybe that's what was happening this week. Maybe it was just the first time she'd been with her dad long enough for her moods to affect them.

It didn't matter. Today was going to be a good day. Today was going to be a great day. She was getting picked up later this evening by Coach Dawn and Quinn, and they would drive together to Brooklyn for the New York Liberty basketball game. Her dad gave her money for snacks and Mom had surprisingly given her money for a souvenir, and she and Quinn were going to sit together and watch a basketball game.

She was practically buzzing, her phone tucked tightly into her hands as she waited for Quinn to text her that they were outside. She already had her sneakers on and was wearing an old Liberty T-shirt that she'd gotten for Christmas ages ago and didn't fit so great anymore.

Her dad glanced out the kitchen window. "I think Dawn is pulling up—"

Harbor leapt out of her seat before he could even finish. "Bye, Dad, see you later!"

"Be good, have fun!" he called after her.

In her excitement, she slammed Dawn's car door a little harder than she meant to. "Yikes! Sorry!"

Coach Dawn laughed. "You ready?"

Harbor turned to look at Quinn. She had her hair down, the blue tips brushing her shoulders. She had on a Liberty jersey, and she smiled big, right at Harbor. "I'm ready," Quinn said quietly.

Much, much more loudly, channeling her inner Cordelia, and even her inner Boom, Harbor said, "Yes! I'm so ready!"

It was Harbor's dad who first got her into basketball. He was the only one of her parents who ever played. Mom, though she was athletic and strong, focused on fishing and boats, even when she was little. Mama had played soccer all through school. Harbor had also played soccer for while. Mama would sit on the sidelines and bring orange slices for her team. Eventually, though, basketball took up more and more time so she had to leave soccer behind.

Harbor never thought to wonder if that had bummed Mama out, but she found herself wondering now.

Harbor shook away those thoughts. It wasn't her fault she was better at basketball. Sometimes people just liked one thing more than the other, and it had nothing to do with her dad, or with Mama. It just was who Harbor was.

Right?

As she followed Quinn and Coach Dawn to their seats in the Barclays Center, the bright lights illuminating the basketball court below, Harbor knew that yes, basketball was who she was. "I'm gonna come here one day," she said to Quinn. "But not to watch the game. I'm gonna play in it."

Quinn leaned over to nudge her shoulder into Harbor's. "I'll come watch you play. All the time."

The game was perfect.

The Liberty played the Phoenix Mercury, which meant Harbor got to watch Diana Taurasi. She made a mental note to tell Marina. She made a second mental note to maybe take down the poster at home, which would make Marina happy. She could bring it to her dad's, to the guest room that was her bedroom. And, sure, maybe it was her dad's room, too, for work during the week, but it was only hers at night. Her dad wouldn't mind if she hung a poster. She could make the room feel more like hers. Maybe they could start calling it *her room*, instead of the guestroom.

At halftime, Coach Dawn marched Harbor over to the merchandise stand. "That shirt looks like it's cutting off your arm circulation," she said. It was true. Growth spurts and old Christmas gifts don't really go together. "Let's get you a new shirt that fits."

Harbor put it on over her other shirt immediately. Then she and Quinn got a giant pretzel to share. "Do you want to get cheese to dip it in?"

"I've never dipped my pretzel in cheese before."

"Oh, Harbor," Quinn said. "This is going to rock your world."

The game started again, and Harbor sat with Quinn, sharing a pretzel, dipping it in cheese sauce that did, indeed, rock Harbor's world.

At the final buzzer, the score was 73 to 64. The New York Liberty won, and Harbor and Quinn jumped out of their seats, cheering their heads off. Harbor turned to look over at Quinn, at the big smile on her face. Quinn was jumping and shouting, which was very un-Quinn-like. Unless she was really excited. Like at the fireworks. Like here, at the game. Harbor loved seeing her like this. Harbor loved that she'd seen so many sides of Quinn. She wanted to know everything there was to know about her.

Quinn turned to look at Harbor, too.

For a second, a millisecond, all the noise and the lights and the basketball court faded away as they looked at each other. And then Harbor, her face flushed, quickly looked away.

"That game was awesome," Quinn said. "Today was perfect."

Harbor kept her gaze down at her feet. "Maybe we could do it again sometime."

"Oh definitely," Quinn said.

Harbor took a deep breath and picked her head back up. "When I live with my dad, we can hang out all the time. We can . . . we can go to games or just hang out whenever. Not just on the weekends or with everyone on the team. Just like this." She paused a second. "I mean, if you want to."

Quinn wrapped her arms tightly around Harbor in a hug. Harbor, stunned, took a second before she was able to hug Quinn back.

Quinn's voice was quiet and soft right in Harbor's ear. "I absolutely want to," she said, just for Harbor to hear.

Harbor's face was flushed the entire car ride home.

It was after ten when Harbor got home. She wasn't surprised her dad had waited up for her. He said he would. She was surprised, though, that when she opened the front door, he was sitting on the couch with his phone to his ear.

"Oh, she's here now," he said as Harbor closed the door behind her. "I'll let her know. Just let me know the plan for Sunday. I can keep her another day or two, no problem."

That was weird. She was already staying at her dad's way longer than she ever had before. Why would she need to stay even more?

Weirder, why did her chest clench thinking about having to stay an extra day or two?

"I can tell her. I'll do it now. I'll talk to you later." Her dad hung up the phone and put it down on the coffee table in front of him. "Hey, kid. How was the game? I was going to watch it, but I couldn't find it on TV."

That wasn't surprising. Harbor could only ever find a handful of games on TV each season. "Who were you on the phone with? Mom?"

"Nadia actually."

"What's going on?" Harbor asked.

"Nothing bad. I mean, yeah it's sad. But you don't need to look all anxious, it'll be okay," he said.

"What will?" Harbor asked.

He gave her a cringe of a smile, as though he didn't actually want to tell Harbor this, even if he told Mama he could.

He sighed.

Harbor's stomach hurt.

"Samantha's grandmother passed away this morning."

CHAPTER EIGHTEEN

Samantha's grandmother was old and frail and forgetful. She was the only family Sam had known before the Ali-O'Connors became her family, too. When her grandmother stopped being able to take care of herself, when she'd had to move into the nursing home, she'd stopped being able to take care of Sam, too.

Sometimes Sam talked about how they used to take really long walks together on the boardwalk before she got sick. Sometimes, when Sonny would talk about a recipe he had found, Sam would mention that her grandmother was a really good cook, too.

But that was all Sam really ever said about her.

Harbor met Sam's grandmother once. She'd told Harbor that she really liked her name. She'd quoted a poem with the word *harbor* in it, and Harbor tried to remember who Sam's grandma said the poet was. She tried to remember the words to the poem.

What was that poem?

Harbor felt weird that night at her dad's house, in her bedroom, alone. It was so quiet here, and Harbor worried Marina wouldn't hear Sam over the sound machine if Sam had a nightmare. She thought about texting Mom to keep an ear out, because they probably thought Sam didn't have nightmares anymore. Harbor was always the one who woke up when she did.

It was really late at night, though. She shouldn't text Mom. Sam would be fine. She didn't need Harbor. No one had even asked Harbor to come home.

At least here she'd be able to sleep all night.

Though, she ended up not really sleeping much at all.

When she woke the next morning, she realized she didn't want to be here. "Dad?" she said as he poured himself a cup of coffee.

"You're up early," he said. "I can make you some eggs if you want? I don't have a work meeting for a couple hours still."

"I want to go home," Harbor said. She clenched her teeth so she wouldn't start crying. "Can you please take me home?"

"Is this about Sam's grandmother?"

"I need to be home. With my sister. With Sam," Harbor clarified. It wasn't like her dad didn't refer to her siblings as her siblings, but he didn't really talk about them much at all, either. "And are they having a funeral? I want to go to the funeral. I don't even know what happened. Why did she die?

Did Mom or Sam know she was dying?" *Why didn't anyone ask if I wanted to be there?*

Harbor was pretty sure she was crying now, no matter how hard she clenched her teeth.

"Hang on," her dad said, fumbling with the phone in his pocket, nearly dropping it in the process. "Let me call and talk with your mom."

He quickly explained that Harbor was upset, all in one breath, when Mom answered her phone. He then handed the phone over to Harbor. "Hey, little fish," Mom said. Hearing her voice made Harbor want to cry more. "I'm sorry. I should have asked if you were okay."

Why didn't you?

"We have a lot going on right now, but the funeral is going to be on Sunday. Would it be okay if you went to practice Saturday and then your dad took you to the funeral Sunday morning? He'll talk to your coach for you about missing practice that day. Does that sound okay?"

No. It didn't. Harbor wanted to come home now. What did it matter that they had a lot going on?

But how could she say that, when she was the one who told them she wanted to stay with her dad? She was the one who asked for this.

One of the rules of boating according to Mom, and there were many, was that when you were driving a boat you had to know when it was your job to get out of the way.

Harbor had gotten herself out of the way.

"Yeah," she said. "That sounds okay."

They were scrimmaging. Coach Dawn had the starting five (which did not include Harbor) against the backups (which did.) The first team to score twenty-five points or more would win. Harbor and Quinn, since they played the same position, were paired up with each other.

Quinn was excited about this. "This practice will be so fun," she said in her quiet way, only for Harbor's ears, as they stood face to face for the jump shot. "Good luck."

"Good luck," Harbor mumbled, though she wasn't sure if she actually meant it. It wasn't that she wanted Quinn to play bad, but she wanted herself to play better. She wanted to show Coach Dawn that Quinn wasn't the best, that Harbor could be the best. Even if she *also* wanted Quinn to be happy.

Quinn always smiled when she played.

"Okay," Coach Dawn said. "You two ready?"

"Ready," Quinn said.

Harbor wasn't ready.

The funeral was tomorrow.

Harbor wanted to be home tonight. She wanted her dad to pick her up and take her back home, so she could be there first thing in the morning.

Coach Dawn tossed up the ball, and Harbor, too lost in

her thoughts, was a half second behind Quinn. Quinn tapped the ball over Harbor's head to Geena. Harbor caught Coach Dawn's gaze, and she blushed furiously as she chased the rest of the players down the court.

That was how practice kept going, no matter how hard Harbor tried to keep up. Maybe Quinn was just better. Maybe Harbor would never get to start, and maybe Coach Dawn shouldn't have offered to let Harbor play on her fall AAU team in the first place. What if Harbor just sat the bench at every one of those games? Coach Dawn was the one who started all of this. Harbor would be spending her summer on Sunrise Lagoon, like always, if Coach Dawn hadn't come to her basketball game.

She would be kayaking down the lagoon with Sonny, picking mussels for Mom to clean and Mama to cook in red sauce with linguini.

Lost in her thoughts again, Harbor tripped over her own feet as Quinn jumped up for a layup. Quinn's body slammed into Harbor, and that impact, plus her own feet, had her falling to the floor. The ball went in the basket, because of course it did.

When Quinn offered Harbor a hand to help her up, she didn't take it.

Instead, she started crying.

Coach Dawn blew her whistle and made her way to Harbor. She bent down to try and look into Harbor's eyes, but Harbor kept her gaze down, wiping her cheeks, trying to stop the tears from coming. "Hey, you okay? What hurts?"

Harbor didn't know how to answer Coach Dawn. She hadn't hurt herself when she fell. She didn't know why she was crying. All she knew was that she couldn't stop, and the more she tried the less she could catch her breath, and everyone was staring at her. *Quinn* was staring at her.

"Okay, everyone, take a water break," Coach Dawn said. "Harbor, can you stand up? Come on, walk with me over there."

Coach Dawn helped Harbor up, and Harbor followed her off the court, far away from the bench where everyone else was getting a drink.

"You feeling okay, Harbor?" Coach Dawn asked.

Harbor nodded even though she was still crying.

"Your dad talked to me about a death in the family?" Coach Dawn said. "I'm sorry to hear that."

"It's not . . ." Harbor wiped at more tears. "It's my sister's grandma. I'm not related. Sam's adopted. I've only met her grandma once."

"It's still sad, though, huh?" Coach Dawn said.

"Yeah, I guess."

"Your dad said the funeral is tomorrow. I find funerals really stressful."

"I'm not stressed. I want to be there," Harbor said. "I want to be there for Sam, because her grandma isn't my family, but I'm Sam's family."

Coach Dawn nodded. "Has Quinn ever told you I'm adopted?"

"I want to play, Coach Dawn," Harbor suddenly blurted out. "I want to . . . I don't understand why I'm not starting. Sometimes I barely play. And I don't know what you want from me. I just want to play."

Coach Dawn sighed. "We talked about your role, Harbor. Not everyone can start."

"I don't know what my role is," Harbor said, the tears that were almost stopping starting up all over again. "I have no idea what my role is."

"Tell me about your family," Coach Dawn said.

Harbor blinked at her. She glanced behind her, where the rest of her team was still taking a break. Some of them started shooting the ball around. They were all waiting for Harbor to pull it together. "Um. Well. I have four siblings."

"Okay." Coach Dawn nodded. "You're the oldest?"

"Yeah. And then Sam, but we're the same age. I'm four months older. And then Marina, and then Cordelia and Lir."

"Do you have a role in your family? As the oldest?"

Harbor shrugged. "I mean. I don't know. Sometimes I have to watch my younger siblings and stuff."

"But sometimes you don't, right?"

"Well, yeah. If Sam's home and she does it. Or if my moms are home," Harbor said.

"So, you rotate in, right? When your moms need you to? Or you tag Sam in, instead?"

Harbor sighed. "This is a ridiculous analogy."

Coach Dawn laughed. "Oh yeah? And why's that?"

"Because watching my little siblings isn't playing basketball. And, you know what? Sometimes my family doesn't need me at all. Because there's enough of them," Harbor snapped.

"So what, then? The team sometimes doesn't need me either? Is that what you're trying to say?"

Coach Dawn placed a hand on Harbor's shoulder, giving it a gentle squeeze. "I think you need to take some time and think about that. If you really think the team doesn't need you, then we need to be having a different conversation. Practice is almost over, and I know you're not coming tomorrow, so you have an entire week to do me the favor of thinking about everything you've accomplished with the team this summer. *Really* think about whether or not they need you," Coach Dawn said. "Can you do that for me?"

Harbor sighed. "Yeah. Fine."

"Okay. Go shoot around with everyone else," Coach Dawn said, dismissing her.

Everyone ignored the way Harbor's eyes were still a little wet and her nose was still pretty red. Quinn passed her the ball and offered her a soft smile.

Harbor didn't smile back.

She took the ball and shot it at the net.

CHAPTER NINETEEN

They were running late. Harbor hated being late.

It wasn't her dad's fault or anything. He had actually been awake and dressed and even made Harbor breakfast nice and early that morning. She wasn't all that hungry—her stomach felt a little wobbly—but she picked at the eggs he scrambled for her anyway.

The problem was, they couldn't drive straight to the funeral. They had to go to Harbor's house first, because Harbor hadn't packed anything to wear for a funeral. All she had was shorts and tank tops and basketball clothes. Plus, driving south in New Jersey during the day on a weekend in the summer was the actual worst. *Everyone* drove south in New Jersey on the weekends in the summer. The tourists were trying to get to the boardwalks and beaches.

Which meant there was traffic.

Loads of it.

Harbor and her dad practically crawled down the Garden State Parkway, and by the time they got to Sunrise Lagoon, the rest of Harbor's family had already left for the service.

Her dad parked but kept the car idling while Harbor ran inside. Good Boy immediately ran to the door, though he stopped when he realized it was her. He didn't jump at her like he always did when any of the Ali-O'Connors came home, no matter how long they'd been out.

Harbor didn't have time to wonder why he didn't attack her with kisses. "I can't play with you, I can't walk you, I'm already really, really late, Good Boy!" she said, rushing into her bedroom and closing the door behind her so she could quickly dress in peace.

Mama (she assumed) left a black dress on Harbor's bed. Harbor put it on, but she realized immediately she hadn't worn it in a while. Back before her growth spurt. It fit . . . okay, she supposed, even though it was a little shorter than she was comfortable with.

It was fine, it'd be fine. She didn't have time to worry about it. She ran back out the front door, which slammed behind her. Good Boy stood at the door, looking at her with his sad puppy dog eyes as she climbed back into her dad's car so they could head, finally, to the funeral home.

The service had already started when they arrived. "We can't go in there," Harbor said, mortified. "We're late. Everyone is already in there."

"We'll sit in the back, Harbor, it's fine," her dad said.

He took her hand and they entered together. The service for Sam's grandma was in a small room, and Harbor didn't recognize any of the people. They were all a lot older, maybe friends of Sam's grandma from before she went into the nursing home, or maybe friends of hers from the nursing home. Harbor didn't know. Sam's grandmother was Catholic, so a priest stood at the front, a large picture of Sam's grandmother behind him, as he spoke in a soothing voice about grief and peace and life. For a moment, Harbor couldn't look away from the photograph of Sam's grandmother. It was the first time she realized just how much Sam looked like her.

Harbor and her dad took a seat in the very last row, and Harbor craned her neck to find her family.

They were in the front row. Harbor could hardly see them. Sam was sitting between Mom and Mama, the twins on the other side of Mama, and Marina on the other side of Mom. Mom had an arm wrapped around Sam and an arm wrapped around Marina. The twins looked as though they must be sharing the same chair, they were leaning so closely into Mama.

Harbor's family was a blended family, so they didn't all look like one another. Sam didn't look like Marina, who didn't look like Mom, who didn't look like the twins. From where she was sitting, though, Harbor thought her family looked 100 percent like a family.

Even without her sitting with them.

"'The tide recedes but leaves behind bright seashells on the sand,'" the priest recited. "'The sun goes down, but gentle warmth still lingers on the land. The music stops, and yet it echoes on in sweet refrains. For every joy that passes, something beautiful remains.'"

Harbor swallowed, squeezing her hands together in her lap.

Her dad reached over to place his much larger hand over her own, squeezing before reaching his arm around her to hug her a little closer.

Harbor tried to relax into him.

But what she really wanted was to be up front, sitting with the rest of her family.

When the funeral ended, Harbor found herself blockaded by old people. Everyone wanted to give their best wishes to Sam, to tell Sam how much they loved and adored her grandmother.

Harbor's dad kept telling her to calm down and wait as she tried to shove her way through the crowd.

"Just wait your turn, Harbor," her dad said.

She didn't want to wait her turn. She shouldn't *have to* wait her turn.

When she finally got near her family, Mama saw her first. "Hey, you," she said, reaching over to pull Harbor into a hug. Harbor relaxed in Mama's arms for the first time since her dad told her Sam's grandmother died. "It was really sweet of you to come."

That made Harbor tense up all over again. It was sweet of her to come? Was it sweet of Marina or Cordelia or Lir to come, too? The three of them were still sitting in their seats, and Harbor thought about how if this had happened before this summer, or on a week that she wasn't spending with her dad, she would be sitting there, too, looking uncomfortable and waiting patiently for this whole thing to be over with.

"Hi, Doug," Mama said. "Thanks for coming."

Thanks for coming. It was the same for Harbor's dad as it was for her, and that didn't feel fair. That didn't feel *right*.

At the sound of Harbor's dad's name, Mom turned to them. "Oh! Hey," she said. She leaned at the same time as Harbor's dad, and they did an awkward sort of hug.

Mom smiled at Harbor. "I'm glad you're here," she said, which wasn't as bad as *thank you for coming*, but it still didn't exactly thrill Harbor.

Someone bumped into Harbor from behind and she stumbled. She stepped out of the way.

"Hi."

She hadn't even seen Sam standing there until now. "Oh, hey."

Sam's black dress did fit, because Sam hadn't grown as much. It made Harbor feel older than Sam sometimes, like she really was the big sister.

They stood there, staring at each other for a moment, until someone—another old person—stepped around Harbor to say to Sam, "Ivy was wonderful. And a hoot! She was always so lively. We were all lucky to have known her."

Sam smiled at the woman, but the smile was all teeth (and Sam never smiled with all her teeth).

Then the woman stepped away, and it was just Sam and Harbor staring at each other again.

Harbor knew she should say something. *Sorry for your loss.* That was what people said, right? Or something like, *Your grandma was really nice to me once.*

"Do you remember what the poem was?" Harbor found herself suddenly asking. "The one your grandma told me."

Sam's eyebrows scrunched up. "My grandma told you a poem?"

"Remember? With my name in it."

"'This way, this way, oh heart oppressed, so long by storm and tempest drivin. This way, this way, lo here is rest, rings out the harbor bell of heaven.'" It was Mom who recited it, wrapping an arm around Harbor and Sam both. "I remember."

Harbor watched as Sam leaned into Mom. She looked worn out and tired.

"Do you want to maybe go outside for a bit?" Harbor asked. She needed air—she was sure Sam did, too.

"Actually, we should get ready to go. We have to get to the restaurant before everyone else," Mom said.

They were headed to something sort of like an afterparty of a funeral. Since it was smaller, Mom had arranged for food at a local diner for anyone who wanted share stories about Sam's grandma.

"Want me to grab the twins and Marina?" Harbor asked.

"You're going to go with your dad, so you can go ahead and find him right now," Mom said.

"Oh."

Harbor watched her moms gathered Sam and the rest of her siblings while her dad gathered her. Harbor's dad followed Mom's car to the restaurant, where Harbor wanted to go sit with Sam and Mama and everyone, but she also didn't want to leave her dad alone, so she sat with him.

She watched as Marina sat next to Sam and said something that Harbor couldn't hear, but made Sam laugh softly.

This was what you wanted, Harbor told herself. *This was what you asked for*.

Still. Harbor never thought that wanting some extra space, that wanting to spend more time with her dad, that wanting to play the best basketball she could play, would make her feel like she was nothing except a half sibling.

CHAPTER TWENTY

They'd brought Good Boy home when Harbor was seven. He was small then, though that didn't last very long. His paws were always huge, and he'd trip over them in a way that Harbor could now relate to. His ears were large and floppy, and even though he eventually grew into both his ears and his paws, he'd been a funny looking puppy.

Mama brought him home, in a very un-Mama like moment. He had been wandering around the Shop Rite parking lot alone, chasing seagulls, splashing in the puddles in the asphalt from the rain the night before. Mama was one of the bystanders who stuck around to see if he belonged to anyone. When it was decided that he was by himself, she took him home.

It was supposed to be temporary.

Mama, at least, swore and promised Mom it would be temporary.

They would watch the puppy until they found out if he had owners who were missing him, or until they found him a good home if he didn't.

No one came looking for him. And by the time they realized they would have to find him a home, the entire family had fallen in love with him. Even Mom, who he curled up with on the couch each night, knowing exactly which family member he had to suck up to.

They'd adopted Good Boy into their home, and he'd been family ever since.

Which made Harbor extra frustrated that he was currently ignoring her.

She had gone home with her family after the funeral, where she would stay for the week, like usual. Which meant that when Mom said, "Can someone please take Good Boy out?" and no one else responded, Mom had looked pointedly at her. "Don't think I'm not fully aware that you haven't had to pick up any Good Boy poop for over a week."

Harbor groaned. "Fine. I'll take him."

"Thank you," Mom said, and then promptly went out the back door, where everyone else was hanging out, and now Harbor had to walk the dog because no one else could be bothered.

Fine.

"Come on, Good Boy," Harbor said. "Let's go out."

He lifted his head a bit, before putting it back down.

Harbor sighed. She grabbed his leash and jingled it. That usually got him going.

He cried a little but didn't move.

"You need to go out," Harbor said. The plan was to go for a lagoon ride on one of Mom's boats before dinner, and they didn't want to do that without making sure Good Boy did his business. Otherwise, he might do it in the house, and that was the last thing any of them needed. The last time he did that, it had smelled for a week.

Wanting Good Boy to go outside so she could get this whole thing over with, she slid his collar over his head. She had to pick up his head a little to get it completely onto him. She tugged a little, and he finally got the message and stood up. He stared at her. "Well?" she said. "What are you waiting for?"

He hesitantly followed her to the front door.

He acted this way sometimes when they needed someone from the neighborhood to walk him, if they were out at the beach for a long day or something else came up that kept them away from home all afternoon. He didn't like being taken outside by anyone other than members of the Ali-O'Connor family. Boom had tried to take him out once when it was Marina's turn, and Good Boy had stopped in the middle of the street, refusing to go any farther until Marina took hold of the leash.

Harbor didn't want to admit the dog was hurting her feelings.

But he kind of was.

Once they were outside, he pulled at the leash, wanting to lead the way. They walked over to the edge of the marshes, where he stuck his nose into the tall grass and started sniffing around. When he started chomping at the grass, Harbor tugged a bit on his leash. "Come *on*, Good Boy."

He kept sniffing around.

"Good Boy!" she yelled, which startled him. He jumped back, causing the egrets that were sitting in the marshes a few feet away to flutter their wings and fly out of the way, which startled Good Boy even more. He barked his head off at them, causing them to flutter and move again, which set Good Boy off even more. Harbor tugged at the leash again, which Good Boy did not like, and between Harbor's increasing frustration and the birds, Good Boy, overstimulated and upset, took off after the birds. It was hard enough holding onto his leash when he wanted to go somewhere—he often walked the Ali-O'Connor children more than they walked him—but he was a one-hundred-sixty-five-pound dog who had suddenly started running. Harbor didn't stand a chance holding the leash, and it burned against her hands as she tried. It yanked at her arms, and she fell forward from the weight of it, skimming on her knees on the hard ground and she had no choice but to let go.

With a giant dog barreling toward them, the birds started flying away.

Good Boy kept following them.

"Wait, no! Good Boy, stop!" she called after him. Her knees and palms burned, and she stood up, limping a bit as she brushed at the asphalt on her skin. She started to run after him, but it hurt, and she was bleeding a little and she wiped her knees again before trying again to go after him.

Good Boy was *fast*.

And before Harbor could catch up with him, he turned the corner and disappeared.

"Good Boy!" she called, running in the direction she'd seen him go. "Where are you? Good Boy, come!"

Where could he have gone?

He couldn't have gotten far, right?

But there are cars. And water.

Good Boy can swim though. He'll be fine. Right? She just had to find him.

Good Boy had never run away from an Ali-O'Connor. Not since he was a puppy.

But Harbor wasn't an Ali-O'Connor. Not really, right?

She couldn't go home for help. She couldn't admit to her family that she lost Good Boy, that he had run away from her. She had wanted to leave, to live with her dad, and now her family would thank her for coming to important things like funerals, instead of expecting her to be there, and Good Boy would treat her like a stranger. It was her fault, anyway, wasn't it? It was what she wanted, and she had yelled at Good Boy, and she had made Cordelia cry, and she had failed at the role of big sister.

She couldn't go home for help.

Instead, she found herself knocking on the Badgers' front door.

Sonny opened the door. He seemed super surprised to see her. "Oh," he said, and then his eyes opened wider. "You're bleeding?"

She was. Her knees stung a lot. "I need your help. *Please*, Sonny. I lost Good Boy, he . . . he ran away from me and I don't know where he went and he's a good boy but he's so stupid sometimes and there are cars and please, *please* help me, Sonny."

"Good Boy ran away?" Sonny said. "From you?"

"Yes," she said, clenching her jaw.

He shoved his sneakers on without untying them, joining Harbor on the porch and shutting the door behind him. "Did you tell your family? What way did he go?"

"I can't tell my family. They can't know. I think over that way? He disappeared, and I don't know how a giant dog can just disappear!"

"It's okay, Harbor. We'll find him." Sonny said it with such conviction, like he was so sure, and Harbor hadn't felt that way about anything in a long time. It calmed her down, just a little, because Sonny never sounded sure, ever. He said everything like it was a question, and just knowing that, even though he was as mad at her as he was and should be, he was still willing to help?

Well, that made Harbor breathe a little easier.

"Good Boy!" he called, leading the way until Harbor caught up with him.

"Good Boy!"

"He's not in the road. Maybe he went down into the marshes," Sonny said. "You said something about birds?"

"He was chasing them, yeah," Harbor said.

The sun was starting to make its descent, and Harbor had to shield her eyes with her hands as she squinted out at the marshes, and the water, looking for a giant dog who shouldn't have been so hard to find. Who shouldn't have wanted to run away from her in the first place.

This was all her fault anyway.

She'd yelled at him. She'd also yelled at Sonny.

"I'm sorry I told Sam," Harbor said as Sonny carefully stepped into the wet, swampy marshes, trying to get a better angle to look for Good Boy.

He didn't say anything for a moment. He leaned over, peering at a stretch of tall grass. "Why did you? Tell Sam?"

"I guess I was mad at you."

"Because I like Sam?"

"Because you like hanging out with Sam instead of me," Harbor said. "Because you're my best friend, and instead of wanting to be with me, you just wanted to be with Sam, and everything felt weird, and I wanted it to be like it used to be!"

"You weren't around, Harbor!" Sonny said, before calling out: "Good Boy! Come, Good Boy!" He paused for a moment.

"You had basketball and then you were at your dad's a lot. I wanted to hang with you, too. Just because I like Sam doesn't mean I don't like you. I just don't like you like that? I just like *you*, Harbor. You're like having a Badger sister."

Harbor pulled a face. "I'm not a Badger. *You're* like an Ali-O'Connor."

"Good Boy!"

And then, muffled by the wind and the tall grass, they both heard it. A whine from a dog that they'd heard a million times before. "Good Boy!" Harbor shouted, and he cried from somewhere again, and Sonny and Harbor took off running around another bend.

That was when they saw him. He was out a little too far in the marshes, the water and mud up to his knees. He was dirty and stuck, and he saw Sonny and Harbor and started crying louder and barking his head off. "Good Boy!" Harbor said, running over to him, squashing and splashing as she stepped into the swampy marshes.

"Careful, Harbor!" Sonny said. "Remember when George got stuck that time? Don't get too close to Good Boy or you'll get stuck, too!"

Harbor used one of her long arms to reach as far as she could for Good Boy's collar. She wrapped her fingers around it and tugged, but it didn't matter. Good Boy didn't budge. He was too stuck, and too scared, and Harbor had to admit defeat. "Sonny, go get my moms. Go get help."

"Don't go too far in, Harbor, okay?"

"I won't! Just go get help!"

Sonny took off running, leaving Harbor and Good Boy alone. Harbor got as close as she could. She took another step, and the mud sucked her shoe right off her foot before she could pull it back. She couldn't go any farther. She had a strong grip on his collar, and she tried to use her other hand to pet him, to let him know that she would keep him safe, but she could barely reach his ear with more than just her fingertips.

"I'm sorry, Good Boy," she said. "I'm sorry that I yelled at you and that I'm never home to play with you. I'm sorry that when I'm home I just push you away. I'm sorry you don't love me as much anymore. I promise I'll play with you more. I promise I'll pet you more. Just don't move, okay? Just stay right here and Mom will be here to help us, okay?"

Good Boy looked at her, licking her fingertips. He whined some more, and as she spoke to him, his tail went *wag-wag-wag*, splashing against the water.

"I'm sorry," she said again. "I'm sorry you were alone and scared, but I'm here, Good Boy."

"Harbor!"

She turned her head just in time to see Mom come splashing into the marshes, Mama, Sonny, and Sam all waiting at the edge of the road. "Can you reach them?" Mama called after her.

Mom had a strong hand wrapped around Harbor's arm. She tugged roughly, not realizing Harbor wasn't stuck, yanking

Harbor up and away from Good Boy, even though Harbor fought against it. "Wait, no! I can't let go!"

"I've got him, Harbor, go by Mama."

"No!" Harbor said.

Mom and Harbor both reached for Good Boy, Harbor tugging at his collar, while Mom wrapped her arms around his body and *pulled*. Good Boy licked Mom's face, his tail still wagging. Once his legs were freed from the mud a little bit, he tried to run. At first he didn't go anywhere, just wiggled and wiggled in Mom's and Harbor's grasp, squelching in the mud, until he finally broke free. Mom and Harbor fell back into the water as Good Boy took off toward the road.

Mama, Sonny, and Sam were waiting for him. They grabbed him, and Mama secured his leash.

He was safe.

He was safe, and Mom helped Harbor out of the marshes, and they were safe, too. Good Boy was excited to be free, and he jumped around each of them, still wagging his tail, thrilled by all the attention he was getting as everyone crowded around him.

He pushed his big head against Harbor's belly, and she wrapped her arms around him.

CHAPTER TWENTY-ONE

Mom was outside, attempting to hose Good Boy down before she let him anywhere near the inside of the house. She had hosed Harbor down, too, and would have to hose down herself, but Good Boy was the muddiest—and the hardest to clean—of the three of them. Cordelia and Lir, who loved giving Good Boy a bath, were outside trying to help Mom as they attacked him with soapy rags, and he thought they were just playing with him.

Harbor, wrapped up in a towel, was supposed to shower to actually get cleaned up, but she couldn't stop watching them from the window.

"Hey," Mama said, coming up behind her. She had a bottle of antiseptic. "Can I take a look at your knees, sweetheart?"

They had stopped bleeding, but they still stung.

She let Mama guide her to the couch in the living room, where Harbor sat down and Mama knelt in front of her. She poured some of the antiseptic onto a cotton ball. With her free hand, she gently held Harbor's leg and began dabbing the scrapes.

Harbor hissed when it first made contact, and Mama paused for a moment before continuing.

She wanted to tell Mama about Good Boy. About how this was Harbor's fault. And she wanted Mama to tell her Good Boy still loved her.

Instead, Harbor found herself asking, "When did you first love me?"

Mama looked up from where she was finishing up cleaning one of Harbor's knees. "What?"

"I mean, at first I was just your girlfriend's daughter or whatever," Harbor said.

"Wow," Mama whispered on an exhale. She sat back on her legs. "That feels like forever ago. Though, I guess it also feels like yesterday. You all grow up too quickly."

"But when was it?" Harbor said, not wanting Mama to go off on a tangent about how she missed when they were all little, lamenting they were all creeping too quickly toward becoming teenagers. "When did you first actually love me, and not just because I was Mom's?"

Mama fell quiet for a moment. She focused back on her task, gently cleaning Harbor's other knee. "Sometimes it feels like I've always loved you," Mama said. "But I know that's not what you mean. And I don't know I have an answer for you. There wasn't really a moment where it was like, yes, now I love her. But . . ."

"But?" Harbor said, her voice hushed.

"There was this one time, when you were a baby. You hadn't been walking for very long, but you *loved* being able to walk. You'd wiggle to be put down until your feet hit the floor. And I was spending the afternoon with you and Mom, but she had to leave. A boat was out in the bay and wouldn't start, so she had to tow them in and see what the problem was with the boat this time. Anyway, she left, and it was just you and me," Mama said, dabbing at Harbor's knee. "I think we'd been left alone together before. It wasn't the first time. But I still got a little nervous because I'd never really been around babies before you, not like that, and I loved your mom so much I didn't want to disappoint her by being awful at taking care of you. But then, well, you wiggled and ran and fell into my coffee table."

"Oh, ouch," Harbor said.

Mama smiled up at her. "You had a little silver scar on your forehead for a long time after that." She reached up to push Harbor's hair out of her face. "I don't think it's there anymore. I don't see it, at least. But you screamed, a lot, and it bled, a *lot*, and I cried and called your mom and rushed you to the hospital because I couldn't get it to stop bleeding. It was awful, you just kept screaming and crying and I felt so bad that you were stuck with me and not Mom."

Mama placed a gentle kiss on her knee, finishing the job. "Anyway, when Mom finally got to the hospital, you were all stitched up and fine. Smiley, even. Like nothing had even happened and you didn't have a care in the world." Mama laughed softly. "I broke down crying, though. Instead of soothing you, Mom had to get *me* to calm down, instead."

"Why?" Harbor asked.

"Because I hurt you. Not intentionally, it was obviously an accident. But it was my fault. I thought I maybe should have been watching you better or taken better care of you. Instead, you got hurt, because of me. I felt like I broke you or something."

Harbor smiled. "Well, that's silly."

"Yes. And I know that now. I know that babies, kids, even my stubborn twelve-year-olds"—she winked at Harbor—"they fall and get hurt. We try to make sure you don't, but sometimes we just . . . can't. And I remember saying to Mom, like, 'Wow, this feels awful, this was terrifying, I feel like I'll never feel calm again.' And Mom just held me, laughed a little, and said, in that sarcastic voice of hers, 'Yeah, well, welcome to motherhood.' And that was when it hit me. Like, really hit me. That was when I knew."

"That I was yours?" Harbor asked.

"That I was *yours*, Harbor."

Harbor looked down at her knees. She squeezed her hands together, trying to breathe past the tightness in her chest and the lump in her throat. She wanted Mama to be hers forever. She wanted Good Boy to come running whenever she got home. "Dad calls you Nadia," Harbor said, her throat feeling tight as she tried to talk.

"What?" Mama asked.

"What if I changed my mind? What if I don't know?" Harbor's eyes grew watery, and it didn't matter how much she clenched her teeth, everything felt hard and tight, and her nose started burning. "You told me to figure it out, but what if I don't know? What if I really, really just don't know?"

"Harbor, sweetheart—"

Whatever Mama was going to say, Harbor didn't know. Harbor suddenly, unable to control it anymore, burst into tears. She cried hard and loud and couldn't stop. She cried like Cordelia sometimes cried, like she maybe hadn't cried since she was a little kid, too. She buried her face in her hands, but Mama was suddenly next to her on the couch, pulling Harbor close and nearly into her lap. Harbor didn't remember the last time she was held like this. That was what happened when you grew up and got tall though, right? She was too tall, taller than her moms, the oldest kid in the Ali-O'Connor home, and if she thought Cordelia needed to stop acting like such a little kid, she had no business sobbing into Mama's arms, either.

"Shhh," Mama said into her ear. "I've got you, Harbor. Breathe for me. Talk to me."

But her mama's arms felt so good. She needed this, and she didn't care how old she was. "I'm sorry," Harbor cried. "I don't want you to be just my stepmom."

"I don't want that, either," Mama said.

"I don't want Mom to be mad at me for choosing Dad. I didn't mean to choose Dad over her, I love Mom, I *miss* Mom, I miss fishing with Mom, even though I don't think I want to be a boater like her when I grow up. I loved being with Quinn and my dad on the Fourth of July, but I wished I was here, I wish the summers were the same, I wish me and Sonny were the same, but everything is different now." Harbor pulled back to wipe her face, to try and get herself to breathe. "But I like having my own room and I can't tell Dad I want to leave because he's so happy that I'm there and what if he needs me most?"

"We all need you the most, Harbor," Mama said. "All of us. And I think you feel that really deeply. I think you wanted space, and you wanted to stay with your dad because everyone else got a little too much for you. And there is nothing wrong with that."

The back door opened, and Good Boy came running in, his fur still damp from his hose bath. He ran to sit by Harbor's feet and bump his face into her. She leaned forward to wrap her arms around him, crying harder all over again.

"What's wrong?" Mom said as she rushed into the room. Cordelia and Lir were right behind her, and so was Sam, and then so were Marina and Boom. "What happened?"

Harbor pressed her face into Good Boy's wet, smelly fur. "I don't want to make Good Boy sad. Or Cordelia sad," she said. "I don't want to show up at a funeral after everyone else because everyone else is supposed to be there and I'm not. I wanted to be there for Sam, too. I *liked* Sam's grandma. I liked her a lot."

"Oh, Harbor," Mom said, taking a seat next to her. Her siblings all stood on the edge of the living room, watching her with wide eyes.

"I don't know what I want," Harbor said. "And I know I don't get to choose anyway, that you choose, but I thought I knew. I thought I knew and I don't know how to take it back. It would hurt my dad if I take it back."

"Hey," Mom said. "Listen to me. It isn't your job to worry about how me, or Mama, or your dad feel."

"But I hurt your feelings. I *know* I did," Harbor said. And then she admitted to her moms for the first time, "And Coach Dawn doesn't even start me in games. I don't even play that much. What if I'm not that good and I'm missing summer for nothing? What if I'm wrong about *everything*?"

She buried her face in her hands again, and Mom pulled her close, but Harbor wanted to be held by Mama, too, so she reached out to her, too. She wanted to feel both of her moms and she wanted them to tell her what to do. She wanted them to fix everything for her.

But it wasn't her moms who spoke next. It was Cordelia. "I didn't know you were so sad," she said.

"Hey, all of you, come sit down," Mama said, gesturing to Harbor's siblings who were still standing at the edge of the living room.

"Um, I should go home?" Boom spoke up. "This seems very much like a family thing. And, well, I'm not Harbor's favorite person on a good day so . . ."

Harbor felt herself blushing.

"I don't not like you—I didn't mean—" Harbor didn't know how to explain it. She didn't mind Boom as a person. She was happy Marina had a friend. Everyone deserved to have someone in their corner like Harbor had Sonny. Even if Sonny was mad at her now, he still came and helped her find Good Boy. "You're just *always* here."

"Everyone, come sit down," Mama said again. "You too, Boom."

Harbor didn't like being the center of attention this way. She didn't like that all her siblings (and Boom) sat quietly on the other couch, watching Harbor and her moms to see what was going to happen.

Good Boy rested his head in Harbor's lap. That helped calm her down.

"Okay," Mama said, and then paused, gathering her thoughts. "When I said I wanted you to think about what you wanted, I didn't mean you couldn't talk to us while you tried to figure that out. I know that sometimes you, or your siblings, or even Mom and I, can't figure out what we need. Things can be confusing. Especially for all of you, I think."

"All of us?" Lir asked.

"Yes," Mama said. "Sam and Marina are adopted, and sometimes they feel big emotions about that. And their emotions are different from each other, because their situations were different, too. And you two, Lir and Cordelia, you're growing into great people, but growing up can be scary and weird, I think, and you might have big questions someday, too. Because you're biologically mine, and not Mom's, just like Harbor is biologically Mom's, but not mine. And, still, your situation is different from Harbor's. And I love our big, beautiful, blended family. I love how each and every piece came together. But it still leaves room for a lot of hurt and confusion and things that are hard to figure out."

"Like Harbor wanting to be with her dad?" Cordelia asked.

"Just like that," Mama said.

Mom had been pretty quiet the whole time, and when Harbor looked over at her, she seemed lost in thought, too.

"I want to be here, too," Harbor said.

Mom let out a soft, sad little laugh. "I know, little fish."

"Well, maybe we could, like, rotate the bedroom or something?" Sam spoke up. "Like, maybe, we could take turns sleeping on the couch? So that there's more room sometimes?"

"That's a really sweet offer, Samantha, but we don't want any of you feeling like you need to sleep on the couch," Mom said.

"I don't want to sleep on the couch anyway," Marina chimed in.

"We could share our room?" Lir offered.

"And I told Harbor I wouldn't do experiments anymore. I wouldn't touch her things anymore. We could be better siblings, because Lir and me aren't little kids anymore," Cordelia said. "And then you can just stay here, Harbor."

"We could make sure Marina and I give Harbor more privacy!" Boom spoke up. "My mom says sometimes people need space because I'm loud and obnoxious."

"Oh, Boom," Mama said.

Everyone was being so nice to Harbor. It made her want to start crying all over again. Her shoulders felt heavy, and so did her head, and she suddenly felt very, very tired.

Good Boy licked her face.

"Can I . . ."

"Yeah?" Mom asked.

"Can I just be alone for a bit? Can that be okay?" Harbor asked. "I just . . . want to be alone for a little bit."

"She can have our room," Sam said.

"Please?" Harbor said, turning between her moms.

Mom sighed. She looked like she was going to argue.

But Mama said, "Yes. Go ahead. We can talk more later."

CHAPTER TWENTY-TWO

Harbor was lying in her bed, glancing at her poster of Diana Taurasi and listening to the muffled sounds of her family from behind the closed door. Marina and Sam didn't go anywhere near the bedroom. She listened to the rise and fall of her family's voices and the sound of their footsteps—she could tell Mom's heavy footsteps from Cordelia's and Lir's lighter, faster ones, from the *clickity-clack* of Good Boy's nails.

She kept the light off, and the curtain closed, and she lay there, alone, trying to figure out what she wanted. She liked this: being alone, in her room, but knowing that her family was right outside. It wasn't quiet, like the guest room at her dad's. It was always loud here except for the quiet peace of the early mornings on Sunrise Lagoon.

The sun started to set, and it grew darker and darker in the bedroom. Mama let Harbor eat dinner in her room, which was a first, and when the light fully disappeared, Marina and Sam finally came into the room to get ready for bed.

Harbor hadn't moved. She hadn't touched the sandwich Mama made her, either.

She didn't feel like she'd ever move again. She wanted to just lay here, in the dark, and not have to go to her dad's or play basketball or make any decisions at all.

At some point she fell asleep. She didn't know when. She didn't even remember hearing Marina's sound machine. Morning came, and Harbor didn't get up. She stayed where she was, even when both her sisters climbed out of bed, got dressed, and left her alone again.

Eventually, Mom knocked on the door. When Harbor didn't say anything, Mom cracked it open, popping her head inside. "Harbor?"

"Yeah," Harbor replied.

"Can you get up and get dressed and meet me outside?"

It sounded like way too much to have to do. "I'm tired."

"Please, Harbor?"

Harbor sighed and sat up, looking over at where Mom stood by the door. "Why do you want me outside?"

"Because you look like you could use some fresh air," Mom said. "And because I'd like you to go on the boat with me."

"Why?"

"Because I really want to talk to you, one on one, just you and me," Mom said. "And I know you are well aware, it's very hard to do that in this house."

"Yeah, that's true."

"So . . . you coming?"

"Fine. Yeah, okay."

The twins and Pork were on the back deck when Harbor finally made her way outside. They were attempting to get the kayaks in the water by themselves, and Harbor suddenly realized they were old enough to do that now. Marina and Boom were across the way, laying on towels in Boom's yard with their sunglasses on and tall glasses of lemonade beside them. Sam was sitting cross-legged at the edge of the dock, with a fishing rod in the water.

She looked up as Mom and Harbor approached Mom's boat, *Harbor Me*. "Are you going on the boat?" Sam asked.

"Is it cool if just Harbor and I take a ride?"

Sam nodded quickly, but Harbor interrupted. "Sam can come if she wants."

Mom hesitated for a moment. "Are you sure?"

"Yeah," Harbor said. "I'm sure."

That was how the three of them, Mom, Harbor, and Sam, ended up on *Harbor Me* as Mom sat in the captain's seat, driving them up the lagoon toward the wide-open bay. It was a clear sky, scattered with big puffy white clouds, the sun reflecting on the water. The wind was light, making it easy to cut quickly across the Barnegat Bay. Sam sat on the side seats, and Harbor lounged in the back. They all stared out at the water, at the other boats, quietly watching as Mom drove them past everything.

Eventually, they came to the entrance to the Forked River, where Mom had to cut the engine a bit. There was no wake allowed, which meant boats had to move slowly to prevent making waves that would knock into the boats docked along the houses and restaurants on either side of the river.

The restaurants were already playing loud music that echoed down the river. It made Harbor think about Sonny, who always said he wanted to own a restaurant one day. The kind of restaurant that had good food and good music, that you could drive your boat to if you wanted.

"I don't know if I like Sonny like that," Sam suddenly said. The restaurants must have made Sam think about Sonny, too. It was quiet, but it was loud enough that both Harbor and Mom heard. Mom, though she made a mighty confused face, didn't say anything.

"It's fine if you do," Harbor said. "I don't care."

"I don't know, though," Sam said. "And, like, what if I do? Would that make him my boyfriend? I don't know if I want a boyfriend. But I like hanging around Sonny. He makes me laugh. I think, maybe, I think he's cute?"

"Oh god," Mom said, grumbling a little. "Okay. You are almost teenagers. I'm cool. This is cool. This is fine."

"I think Sonny is the best boy in the whole wide world," Harbor said.

"I'm sorry," Sam said.

"No, Sam, I don't like him like that," Harbor clarified. "I'm just saying. I get it, I guess, if you do."

"Do I have to know now?"

"No," Mom answered. "You can be nice and respectful to Sonny's feelings, while asking him to be nice and respectful to yours. You hear me?"

"Yeah," Sam said.

The whole conversation sat in Harbor's stomach for a moment. She thought about Sonny. About how he always felt like just her best friend.

She thought, then, about Quinn.

About how her friendship with Quinn always felt a little different, and how Harbor really, really didn't know what that meant.

"Mom?" Harbor asked.

"Yeah, little fish?"

"Did Dad get mad, back when you told him you were gay?" Harbor asked. "Did he hate that about you?"

Mom got very, very quiet for a moment.

"Sorry," Harbor said. "Should I not have asked?"

"You can ask me anything, always," Mom said. "It's just . . . a really difficult question to answer. Your dad . . . He's a good person, Harbor. And he was very, very hurt when I left him.

I don't think he's homophobic. He's always been really nice to Mama, I think, all things considered. I hope he's never said anything to you to suggest otherwise. I really hope you'd tell me if he did, but also I think I'd understand if you didn't."

"Oh," Harbor said.

It was kind of a non-answer to a question Harbor thought was fairly straightforward.

"I kind of want to know why you're asking," Mom said. "I just . . . It's a big question to ask."

"I made a new friend. On the basketball team," Harbor found herself explaining. Though, she stopped there, because she didn't know how to keep going. She didn't really know what she wanted to say.

"What's their name?" Sam asked.

"Quinn. Her hair is dyed blue on the ends. And she's really quiet. She only says what she means, and she doesn't mind sitting in silence if you don't want to talk. And she doesn't ask nosy questions about things you don't want to answer. And she's really, really good at basketball. She starts in my position. I hate that I don't start, but I like watching her play." Harbor felt her cheeks blush when she realized how much she had to say about Quinn.

"She sounds cool," Sam said.

"She is," Harbor said.

They all fell quiet again as they continued down the river.

The farther they went, the music from the restaurants got quieter and quieter.

"Hey, you two? You know Mama and I would love you no matter what, always, right? Who you are now, or who you become, we'll always love you. Every part of you. And you don't need to worry about that with us, ever," Mom said. "You both know that, right?"

"Yeah," Sam said. "I know that."

"Good," Mom said, smiling at Sam. "Harbor?"

Harbor knew that, too. Or, at least, it was something she had heard from them before and always wanted to believe. "And Dad?" Harbor asked.

Mom fell quiet again. Mom, like Cordelia, wasn't often quiet. If she was in a room, you always knew she was there. She had a presence that wasn't still or calm or quiet. So every time she was that way, it freaked Harbor out.

But Mom finally spoke again. "You remember how I told you how when you were a baby, it was always just you and me, for a while? You and me and the water."

"Yeah."

"Back then, before I met Mama, before your dad and I split up, I swore I would never let you feel like I was feeling then. That I would do everything I could to make sure you were never as lost as I was. And I know that's hard to understand, because your dad was one of my best friends, and it was hard for me to understand, too. I don't want to upset you thinking about that, about your dad and I splitting up." Mom ran a hand through her hair, looking a little frazzled. "It sucked. It did. I didn't want to hurt him, I was hurting, it was just . . . a lot. But through all that, even when he wasn't around as much at first to be your dad, he always loved you a lot, little fish. He lights up when he sees you. And I don't know if me being gay screwed with his idea of things. And I don't know how he feels about everything. But I do know he's a good person, with a big heart, who has always loved you. I think there's a lot you and your dad need to talk about, though. He needs to know how you feel, right?"

Harbor shrugged. "Yeah. I guess so."

"You're old enough to have an honest conversation about how you feel about living with him, and about Mama, and anything else you want to say to him. And if you need me to talk to him about this, or anything else, you know I will. I'm in your corner, Harbor."

"I'm in your corner, too," Sam said.

Harbor swallowed around the lump in her throat. She didn't want to talk about that anymore, about her dad, or about Quinn.

"I'm in your corner, too, Sam," Harbor said. "And I'm sorry I wasn't here when your grandma died. I really wanted to be. I thought she was great."

Sam's nose grew red, like it often did when she was trying not to get upset. "Thanks."

"Oh, my girls," Mom said as she wiped her cheeks. "Get up here, Harbor. Come drive this boat for me, will you?"

Harbor got up and came around to stand at the steering wheel. Mom stayed close behind her, an arm braced around her like she would do when Harbor was really little and wanted to drive the boat. She didn't need Mom to do that anymore, but she didn't ask her to let go, either. Sam came to stand with them, and Mom wrapped an arm around her, too.

Sam would probably grow up to be the better boater.

That was okay, though.

Harbor still drove the boat the rest of the way back home.

CHAPTER TWENTY-THREE

When Sam and Harbor went to their bedroom to get changed out of their bathing suits, Boom and Marina were already there, playing on Boom's phone. Boom nearly leapt up off her spot on the floor beside Marina's bed, standing to attention. "Oh! Hello! I am going to leave now!"

Harbor rolled her eyes. "You don't need to leave, Boom."

"Oh. Are you sure?"

"Sam and I can take turns getting dressed in the bathroom."

"Oh! Okay! Sounds good!"

Harbor grabbed her clothes, getting ready to head toward the bathroom and ignore Boom and Marina for as long as she could, but she stopped at the doorway. "I like you fine, Boom. Just so you know. I just get annoyed at you the same way I get annoyed at Marina."

Boom tilted her head to the side, not unlike Good Boy. "The same as Marina?" Boom asked. "So, like family?"

"Sure, Boom. You annoy me just like the rest of my family."

"Cool!" Boom said.

Harbor made eye contact with Marina, who smiled at her.

"Yeah," Marina said. "Cool."

Harbor rolled her eyes again, grabbing her clothes and heading out the door to get changed. She didn't get very far. The moment she stepped into the hallway, she tripped over Cordelia, who was inexplicably crawling around on the floor. "*Cordelia!*" Harbor shouted as she fell to the floor hard on her scraped knees. It hurt, a lot, and Harbor turned around to ask Cordelia why she was on the floor like Good Boy.

But Cordelia was already scrambling to stand back up, her eyes wet and wide. "I'm sorry!"

Lir came running out of the twins' bedroom. "She was helping me. I thought I saw a spider. She was looking for it. I asked her to."

Out of the corner of Harbor's eye, she saw the spider. Harbor took the torn toilet paper from Cordelia's hand to grab it. "I got it," Harbor said, squishing it in her hand as she walked past the twins to flush it down the toilet in the bathroom.

Lir looked relieved. "Thank you."

Harbor turned around to see Cordelia still looking anxious.

"It's not your fault I've been staying at my dad's," Harbor said. "I mean, you drive me bonkers and it's annoying when you touch my things. But that's not why. Okay?"

Cordelia slowly nodded. "Oh."

"Okay," Harbor said, walking into the bathroom and moving to shut the door behind her.

"Then why?" Cordelia asked. Lir was standing next to her, looking just as eager to hear the answer.

Harbor thought really, really hard about that question.

She'd been asking herself the same thing a lot, lately.

"I just needed space. And I wanted to play basketball," Harbor said. "And then a whole lot of stuff happened."

Cordelia and Lir both nodded their heads.

Harbor, thinking the conversation was over, went to shut the bathroom door again.

"I still don't like when you're gone," Cordelia said quickly.

"Me either," Lir agreed. "It's weird. Does it feel weird to you?"

"Maybe, sometimes, but . . ." Harbor shrugged. "He's my dad."

The twins grew quiet again. If Harbor was going to get a chance to be in the bathroom alone to finally get dressed, now was the time. Still, looking at the two of them, she wasn't exactly ready to end the conversation, either.

"But," she said, and the two of them looked up at her so eagerly, she felt the lump in her throat all over again, "I like being here with you two, mostly. Some of your experiments,

Cordelia, are pretty cool. Like when you made Frankencrab last summer, before it got gross and started falling apart. And, well, maybe during the week we can go kayaking together or something. Usually, I go with Sonny and Sam. But since you can use the kayaks now, too, maybe we can all go together."

"Lir is really fast on the kayak," Cordelia said. "So, maybe we should race."

"Winner has to do the dishes that night," Lir said.

Harbor figured s he would let them win. "Sounds good."

Cordelia hesitated a minute longer, before she wrapped her arms around Harbor's middle. Lir followed right behind her, and Harbor, although they were so annoying, let them hug her.

She even hugged them back.

Everyone was home Friday evening, when it was time for Harbor to gather her things so Mom could drive her to her dad's house. Harbor wished they weren't. She wished it was a nice, sunny summer day, not a rainy one, so everyone wouldn't be trapped inside.

It felt like her siblings were trying *not* to watch, while also one hundred percent watching.

"Harbor! Shake a leg, we need to get going," Mom said.

Harbor had been moving exceptionally slow. She didn't want to look too eager to go to her dad's house. She also didn't feel so great about going at all.

Mama noticed. "Okay, come here," she said, pulling Harbor close. "You'll be back Sunday night. Go play some excellent basketball and spend some time with your dad. We'll all be here when you get back. There's still so much summer left."

"I have a basketball game on Sunday," Harbor said.

"Oh yeah? I hope you all play great and win, then."

"I don't play all that much," Harbor said. "I mean, I don't know how much I'll play, so . . ."

"You know that's okay, right? That's why you're on this team. To grow as a player. That was the point. You don't have to start, or to play the most minutes, to learn how to be a better player," Mama said. "I'm still proud of you."

"Even though sometimes it's a huge bummer not to play as much as you want," Mom said.

"Right, yeah," Harbor said. "But I mean, it'd be a long drive to maybe not even see me play all that much but . . . I thought maybe, you'd come? To see the team? And me?"

"Of course we'll come," Mama said.

"Honestly, Harbor, the only reason we haven't yet is because we didn't think you wanted us to," Mom admitted. "Maybe that's my fault. Maybe I was just . . . projecting."

Harbor shrugged. "I'm not sure I did want you there. But I do for this game. Okay?"

Mama hugged Harbor tightly. "We'll be there. You have a good weekend, okay?"

"Okay," she said, resting her head for a moment on Mama's shoulder.

"Have fun at your dad's, Harbor!" Sam said.

The twins seemed to follow her lead. "Yeah! Have fun!"

"When you come back, we're gonna go on the kayaks! You said so!"

"You can't back out!"

"I won't," Harbor said. She turned to face Marina. "Boom can have my bed while I'm gone. If she wants."

"Really?" Marina said excitedly.

"But you have to wash the sheets before I get home! I mean it!"

"Okay!"

Good Boy was waiting at the door. Whenever anyone was about to head out, he thought that meant he got to go out, too. His tail was wagging, and Harbor made her way over to him, wrapping her arms around his giant head. She let him lick her face before she pulled away.

"Okay. We really gotta hit the road. You ready?" Mom said.

"Yeah. I'm ready."

Good Boy watched from the door as Mom and Harbor walked to Mom's car. Harbor tossed her bag in the back seat and, out of the corner of her eye, saw Pork and Sonny Badger along the side of the road. Pork was riding his brother George's old electric scooter. Sonny was jogging next to him on the side of the road that led into the marshes, probably to make sure the littlest Badger didn't fall in. They'd had enough excitement with those marshes yesterday.

"Mom, hang on, I need two more seconds," Harbor said. "I just need to go talk to Sonny quick!"

"*Hurry*, Harbor."

"I will!"

Harbor quickly ran toward the Badger brothers. It took her a little bit to catch up, but luckily, Pork wasn't all that skilled on the scooter. He kept starting and going fast and then stopping.

"Sonny!" Harbor called, and Sonny turned around. He grabbed the back of Pork's shirt and tugged a little so that Pork wouldn't start up the scooter again.

"Is everything okay?" Sonny asked, as Harbor made her way to him.

"Yeah. I mean, I wanted to say thanks for helping. With Good Boy. You were a lifesaver."

Sonny shrugged. "Oh, I mean. Of course? I love that big doofball."

And then they both stopped talking and just kind of stood there. Sam always called this Awkward Standing. It usually happened at the start of the summer, when Harbor and Sonny hadn't seen each other for an entire school year and needed to reacclimate to being best friends.

It hurt a little that it was the middle of the summer, and they were still feeling this way.

"I don't know what to do," Harbor said.

"About what?"

"I want to be your friend, Sonny. I think I've been doing a bad job, and I don't know how to make things feel normal again," Harbor said.

Sonny sighed. "Yeah, me, too."

"Why don't you just hang out?" Pork spoke up. "Just be friends? I don't think it's very hard."

It didn't feel all that easy.

"When George got older, a lot of his friends changed. It was weird for him, because some of his friends didn't want to be his friend anymore, and everyone kind of grew in different directions, I guess. That's what my mom said. She said it sometimes happens, because when we get older, we change. Sometimes because we change, we don't make good friends anymore," Sonny said. "But I think we can still make good friends. I don't think we've changed that much. Do you?"

Harbor thought about that. She thought about how much she missed spending time with Sonny on the water. She thought about how, even though he was angrier at her than he'd ever been before, he still helped her find Good Boy. "I don't think we've changed too much, either."

"Maybe we can just . . . start over? When you get back from your dad's, we can pretend Monday is the first day of the summer, and we can just . . . start being best friends like always?" Sonny asked.

"I told Cordelia and Lir we would go kayaking with them," Harbor said. "They want to race us."

Sonny smiled. "So, we race them."

"We should probably let them win."

"Oh, they're going to beat you," Pork said. "Lir is *very* fast."

"Harbor!" Mom called. It echoed over the marshes, causing a few seagulls to pop out of the tall grass and fly away. "Come on, we gotta get going!"

"I'll see you Monday?" Sonny asked.

Harbor smiled. "Yeah. I'll see you Monday."

CHAPTER TWENTY-FOUR

Mom pulled into Harbor's dad's driveway. They'd been driving mostly in silence. Mom had the windows down, which usually made Harbor's ears pop as they drove down the highway, but she liked the white noise of the wind mixed with Mom's pop rock radio station. It reminded her of Marina and her sound machine.

Mom didn't turn off the car, which usually meant she wasn't planning on walking Harbor to the front door. Which was fine. She mostly didn't, anyway. But Mom just sat there and didn't say anything, and Mom would usually be the first to say goodbye.

Harbor hesitated, her hand on the doorhandle as she watched Mom carefully. Mom had her gaze fixed on Harbor's dad's house. "Um. I'll see you Sunday? For the game, right?"

"Yeah," Mom said, finally looking at Harbor and smiling. "Hey, listen. You should talk to your dad this weekend. I think you should tell him how you feel—he deserves to know. You deserve that, too."

It made her feel a little nauseated. "Yeah. Okay."

"And I think you need to hear me say this again. You don't need to worry about me, Harbor. I'm not going to lie. It bums me out when you spend time away from me. And, if I could make all my decisions selfishly? I'd keep you with me, and just me, forever. I can't help feeling like that, I'm human, you know? And I love you. But those are *my* selfish feelings. And if I made you feel like you hurt my feelings for wanting to spend more time with your dad, if I helped make you confused about all this? I'm sorry. Really. And you don't need to worry about me." Mom reached out to tug gently on Harbor's ponytail. "You don't need to worry about your dad, either. We're the adults here, Harbor. We've got this, okay? We both just want the best for you."

"Okay."

"Yeah? Okay?"

"Yeah."

"Okay," Mom said, and then shook her head. "Come here, can I have a hug?"

Harbor gave her a really big one. She didn't remember when she was a baby and it was just her and Mom against the world.

But in moments like these, when it was just her, and Mom, and her mom's arms wrapped around her? She thought that maybe she remembered it, after all.

"See you Sunday, Harbor."

"See you Sunday, Mom."

The first thing Harbor's dad did was ask what Harbor wanted to order for dinner. Her stomach was feeling a little swirly and weird, like the ocean right before a really big storm, so food was the last thing on her mind. "Whatever you want," she said.

"You sure?"

"Yeah, I'm sure."

"Maybe Chinese takeout again?"

Oh, Harbor did *not* think that would sit well in her stomach right now. "Yeah, sure. That's fine."

They sat on the couch together as they waited for the food to be delivered. Some sitcom was playing on TV that made her dad laugh. He'd laugh, and Harbor would remember she was supposed to laugh, too, even though she wasn't paying attention. She didn't know how to have an Important Conversation. Did you just . . . start? Did you have to wait for the right moment? Did you need to be talking about something else entirely and find a way to sneakily bring up the actual thing you wanted to talk about?

Just open your mouth and say something, Harbor.

"Dad?"

The doorbell rang. The food was here.

"Hold that thought, lemme grab that," her dad said.

By the time they had the food spread out on the kitchen table—her dad liked to order a *lot* of Chinese food to share—Harbor was fidgeting. Maybe she didn't need to worry about having this conversation now. Maybe she could just eat her dinner, watch a movie, go to bed, and worry about it tomorrow or Sunday instead.

"I have to learn to cook a few more meals," Harbor's dad said between his mouthful of lo mein as Harbor used her fork to move the food around her plate. "It's been too much takeout for you probably. I know Nadia makes a lot of really great meals for you guys, right? I mean, I know your mom can't cook to save her life unless it involves fileting a fish and chucking it onto the grill."

He laughed.

Harbor didn't.

"I don't like when you do that."

Her dad reached for the container of beef and broccoli. "Make fun of your mom's cooking? I'm sorry. I just meant it as a joke, I used to pick on her all the time but only because she knew I was just as awful in a kitchen as she was."

"No. I mean about Nadia." Harbor felt her face flush. "I mean, about Mama. You always say 'Nadia and your mom' or, 'Is your mom coming to pick you up?' and you just mean

Mom, just one mom. And I have two. Nadia—*Mama*—is my mom, too."

"Oh," her dad said.

That was all he said.

"I'm sorry if that's weird. But I love her an awful lot, and it hurts my feelings when you say she's not my mom, too."

Harbor's dad put his fork down. He stared at his plate for a moment before leaning in to look at Harbor. "You know, the first time I met her? Nadia had never been on a boat before. Not once. She had on this fancy wrap around skirt thing and sandals with *heels*, and I thought, 'Chelsea is going to eat this girl alive.' I didn't think it'd last. Chelsea and I had always been two peas in a pod, ever since we were young, and this new woman was way too different than us." He paused and then laughed. "I was surprised when she held her own. She caught a fish, and Chelsea made her take it off the pole herself. And she did it, too! Fish guts everywhere! But what really got me was how easy Chelsea went on her. She didn't drive the boat as fast as she normally would, she put the killifish on the hook for Nadia, even though your mom always makes everyone do that themselves for the first time so she could laugh at them. At least, she laughed a lot at me the first time. That's kind of when I realized, okay, maybe Nadia will be sticking around after all."

"Oh," Harbor said, not really sure why he was telling her this.

"I didn't warm up to her for a bit. I mean, why should I have, right? I was still pretty sad about the divorce. But then I saw Nadia with you. And, sure, I was jealous. But also, I don't know. She's always been really great with you, Harbor, and I don't want you to think that I don't appreciate her place in your life, and everything she's done for you. Your mama . . . she's a good person. And I'm sorry. I didn't realize I was upsetting you. I didn't even realize I was doing it."

Harbor nodded, looking down at her food.

"Are we okay?" her dad asked.

"Dad I . . . I like being here with you, I do. Really! And I know you like spending time with me, that it's different now than when I was little and you worked a lot. And I like spending time with you, too! I like being here with you, too, because I love you, too, just like I love Mama, and Mom, but . . ." Harbor took a deep breath. "But I don't think I want to stay here all the time. I like being at home, at Sunrise Lagoon. I like being a big sister, and I like being on the water. I like playing basketball with you, Dad, but I can't stay here all the time. I can't, I'm sorry, I'm really sorry."

"Jeez, Harbor," he said, shifting his chair so he was closer to her.

She wiped her cheeks, tears suddenly spilling down, and her dad reached for her hand. "I'm okay. I miss you like crazy when you're not here, but I'm okay."

"But I want you to have someone to play Scrabble with, too."

He laughed. "I don't really know what that means, but, well . . . you're not here all the time, Harbor. I've actually . . . maybe, sort of, got someone to play board games with. I guess I should have told you. I just didn't know how."

Harbor blinked at him. "What? Who?"

He ran a hand over his hair, sheepishly. "Uh. Well. Dawn and I have sort of been hanging out a lot lately, believe it or not."

"*Coach* Dawn?"

"She was my friend before she was your coach, don't forget."

Harbor *had* forgotten. And, when she thought about it . . . Dawn was the one to invite Harbor and her dad to the Fourth of July. When Quinn came over to hang out, Dawn had stayed for dinner, too.

It was funny that her dad had enjoyed spending time with Dawn just like Harbor enjoyed spending time with Quinn.

You still need to talk to him about Quinn, Harbor remembered. *And about Mom, when she came out as gay.*

"I love when you stay with me, kid," Harbor's dad said, tearing Harbor from her thoughts. "And I'd love to have you here more, okay? I would. I always will. The offer is always going to be there. But I'm okay if you stay with your moms. You don't need to make decisions like that just because of me."

Harbor smiled at him.

She still needed to tell him how much she liked being around Quinn. She still needed to know if he would love her, no matter what, while she figured out exactly what *no matter what* meant.

But that was the thing, wasn't it? She had already had the big conversations with her dad, and she didn't yet know why she liked hanging out with Quinn, why she liked watching Quinn play basketball. She didn't have to figure out everything at once, did she? She could save some conversations for later, couldn't she?

"Thanks, Dad," Harbor said.

"Love you, kid," he said. "How about we clean up and find a movie to watch, huh?"

Harbor decided for now, she would save those conversations for later. She was good with the rest for now. "Sounds good."

Harbor loved the sound of basketballs. Whether it was the bounce against the court, or the clang against the backboard, or the swish through the net, she loved it. The squeak of sneakers, the feel of the ball in her hands. Harbor *loved* basketball.

"Coach Dawn?" she asked at the beginning of practice on Saturday.

"What's up, Harbor?" Coach Dawn smiled at her.

Harbor almost made a face thinking about Coach Dawn being *friends* with her dad. But also, she kind of liked it.

"I was thinking, about what you said? About my role on the team?"

"Oh yeah?"

"Yes. And, well, I still think it sucks I don't start, and I do think you could play me more, but also, I know I still need to work on my footwork and on making my free throws," she said.

All of this was true. She was getting better, though. Coach Dawn had been helping her.

"But also, I know that when I go in after Quinn, it gives Quinn a break, which is good. And, if we're down a bunch of points and I come in, I've been on the bench watching from the sidelines and see things a little differently, so I can help in ways that maybe Quinn can't while she's playing," Harbor said. "And it doesn't mean the team doesn't need me, because they do. You can't play with only five people."

"You cannot," Coach Dawn said. "You need the whole team."

Whether it was basketball, or her family, Harbor believed that was true.

"I'm going to get better at my free throws, though," Harbor said. "I'm gonna get better at everything and then you'll have to play me more."

Coach Dawn laughed. "Sounds good, Harbor. I'll hold you to that. Now why don't you go find Quinn and warm up."

Harbor put on her basketball shoes and grabbed a ball. Quinn's face lit up when she saw her, and Harbor felt warm. Maybe Quinn liked hanging out with Harbor, maybe Quinn liked watching Harbor play, as much as she did.

"Hi," Quinn said.

"Hi," Harbor replied.

"You want to shoot?"

"I'm not going to stay for the school year," Harbor said suddenly. Quinn's face fell, and Harbor continued speaking quickly to keep Quinn from looking so sad. "I mean, I'm gonna play the rest of the summer, but I'm not going to stay with my dad all year. I want to be home, with my family. And I'm sorry. I know you really wanted to be on my team."

"It's okay," Quinn said slowly. "I understand. I miss my brother a lot. I bet you miss your siblings a lot, too."

"I do," Harbor said. "Even though they make me crazy." Harbor shot the basketball. She smiled when it went in, nothing but net. "Maybe you can come meet them sometime? It's not the woods, but I think you might like Sunrise Lagoon."

"Will you come back next summer?" Quinn asked.

"Absolutely," Harbor said. "You're not getting rid of me."

Quinn looked relieved. "Oh good."

They didn't talk much after that, but that was fine. That was perfect. They just enjoyed each other's company, trading the basketball back and forth, taking turns making shots and getting the rebounds, until Coach Dawn blew her whistle and started practice.

CHAPTER TWENTY-FIVE

The Ali-O'Connor family was *loud*.

They all sat together in the very last row of the bleachers in the gym. Mom and Cordelia cheered the loudest, bouncing up and down in their seats, even though Harbor hadn't gotten to play yet. Mama had her arms wrapped around Mom's, shouting excitedly anytime someone scored. Sometimes she even shouted for the wrong team, which would have had Harbor rolling her eyes if hadn't been so happy to see them.

A whole row, cheering for her.

No one else's family was as loud as Harbor's.

It was so annoying.

Harbor, though she wouldn't admit it to them, loved it.

Her dad was there, too. Not with the rest of her family— he stood alone on the side of the court by the edge of the bleachers. He wasn't as loud as the rest of them, but he cheered on Harbor's team, too.

Finally, *finally*, Coach Dawn looked down the bench to make eye contact with Harbor. "All right, Harbor," she said. "You're in for Quinn."

Harbor jumped up really quickly. Her family, from the bleachers, started losing their heads.

"Go, Harbor!"

"You've got this, Harbor!"

"KICK BUTT, HARBOR!"

Quinn's face was bright red and she was breathing really heavy when she passed Harbor, bumping fists on her way out of the game. "Awesome job, Quinn!" Harbor said.

Quinn smiled at her. She tugged once on Harbor's jersey before Harbor could get too far away. "Get out there and kill it, Harbor."

Harbor was smiling now, too.

As she jogged by Camryn to get into place, she noticed Camryn was staring at Harbor's family in the bleachers. "Sorry my family's so loud."

"Oh, no, definitely bring them to all our games," Camryn replied. "They make me feel so popular."

Harbor got into position. She'd been paying close attention from the sidelines. Observe and listen. That was what Harbor had learned from Quinn. And while observing, Harbor knew that with their zone defense, there was a small pocket of space the other team kept leaving wide open.

So, when she finally got to play, she found that wide open spot and called out that she was open. Camryn passed her the ball, and Harbor planted her giant feet, which hadn't been feeling quite so big lately. Harbor immediately reached up to take a shot. The girl who tried to block her was much smaller than she was, and she smacked Harbor on the arm instead of the basketball. The referee blew his whistle. A foul.

Harbor had to shoot free throws.

There was a hush as Harbor lined up her shot. She closed her eyes and listened to the silence.

And then Cordelia yelled, "Go, Harbor!"

And Mom said, "Go, Harbor!"

And her dad said, "Don't forget to follow through."

And Mama said, "You've got this!"

And Harbor believed she did.

She took her shots and made them both.

ACKNOWLEDGMENTS

[2 pages TK]

MORE UNFORGETTABLE STORIES FROM
NICOLE MELLEBY
ABOUT COURAGE, HOPE, LOVE
AND WHAT MAKES A FAMILY

Elizabeth Melleby Welch

NICOLE MELLEBY, a New Jersey native, is the author of highly praised books for young readers, including the Lambda Literary finalist *Hurricane Season*, *Camp QUILTBAG* (co-written with A. J. Sass), and *Sunny and Oswaldo*. She lives with her wife and their cats, whose need for attention oddly aligns with Nicole's writing schedule. Visit her online at nicolemelleby.com.